The Books of Nancy Moser

www.nancymoser.com

Contemporary Books

An Undiscovered Life

Eyes of Our Heart

The Invitation (Book 1 Mustard Seed)

The Quest (Book 2 Mustard Seed)

The Temptation (Book 3 Mustard Seed)

Crossroads

The Seat Beside Me (Book 1 Steadfast)

A Steadfast Surrender (Book Steadfast)

The Ultimatum (Book 3 Steadfast)

The Sister Circle (Book 1 Sister Circle)

Round the Corner (Book 2 Sister Circle)

An Undivided Heart (Book 3 Sister Circle)

A Place to Belong (Book 4 Sister Circle)

The Sister Circle Handbook (Book 5 Sister Circle)

Time Lottery (Book 1 Time Lottery)

Second Time Around (Book 2 Time Lottery)

John 3:16

The Good Nearby

Solemnly Swear

Save Me, God! I Fell in the Carpool
(Inspirational humor)

100 Verses of Encouragement — Books 1&2
(illustrated gift books)

Maybe Later (picture book)

I Feel Amazing: the ABCs of Emotion (picture
book)

D1598296

AWN

Historical Books

Where Time Will Take Me (Book 1 Past Times)

Where Life Will Lead Me (Book 2 Past Times)

Pin's Promise (novella prequel Pattern Artist)

The Pattern Artist (Book 1 Pattern Artist)

The Fashion Designer (Book 2 Pattern Artist)

The Shop Keepers (Book 3 Pattern Artist)

Love of the Summerfields (Book 1 Manor House)

Bride of the Summerfields (Book 2 Manor House)

Rise of the Summerfields (Book 3 Manor House)

Mozart's Sister (biographical novel of Nannerl Mozart)

Just Jane (biographical novel of Jane Austen)

Washington's Lady (bio-novel of Martha Washington)

How Do I Love Thee? (bio-novel of Elizabeth Barrett Browning)

Masquerade (Book 1 Gilded Age)

An Unlikely Suitor (Book 2 Gilded Age)

A Bridal Quilt (novella)

The Journey of Josephine Cain

A Basket Brigade Christmas (novella collection)

When I Saw His Face (novella)

When I Saw His Face

ISBN 13: 978-1-7368108-6-6

Published by:
Mustard Seed Press
Overland Park, KS

This story is a work of fiction. Any resemblances to actual people, places, or events are purely coincidental.

All Scripture quotations are taken from The Holy Bible, King James Version

Front cover design by Mustard Seed Press

Printed and bound in the United States of America

When I Saw His Face

NANCY MOSER

Overland Park, KS

Chapter One

Chancebury, England, August 30, 1807

The carriage pulled away from the church. The wedding guests waved and cheered as the bride and groom began their new lives together.

Esther Horton raised her hand to wave, but returned it to her side before the action could be completed. "Petunia didn't even say goodbye."

The words were said for her own benefit, but overheard by her brother-in-law. "You expected otherwise?"

"Hoped otherwise."

Clarence put an arm around her shoulders. "You've done well with her since Stephen died."

"Well enough?"

He shrugged. "Petunia has always owned her own mind."

"Which she does not hesitate to share with others."

"Often and vociferously."

They shared a resigned smile and looked in the direction the carriage had gone.

"Will they be happy?" Clarence asked.

"I pray it will be so," Esther said.

"But?"

Esther fingered the fringe on her shawl. "I expect Petunia will make her husband quite. . ." She didn't wish to say the word.

"Miserable?"

There was a disconcerting satisfaction in having someone else understand the situation. "We both know if making people miserable is a talent, Petunia can easily be considered a girl with unparalleled expertise."

Clarence chuckled. "'For better or worse,' she is John's problem now."

"If it goes badly, it's your fault. You introduced them when she visited you last spring."

He sighed. "May she become his blessing."

They watched as the wedding guests dispersed and Pastor Wilkins closed the doors of the church. The wedding was over. The task fully accomplished.

Esther sighed. "Now what?"

"What, you say?" Clarence asked.

She hadn't realized she'd spoken the words aloud. "Nothing." She took his arm. "Walk me home."

After a dozen steps, he said, "You should move back to Manchester with Sarah and me. Your parents have died, and with Petunia moving to London, there's nothing to keep you here in tiny Chancebury. It was Stephen's choice to move here. I never understood why the countryside was always a lure to him."

"It's a fine village. We were happy here. I *am* happy here."

"So you say, but it's not like you were born here."

"I believe living in a village for eighteen years provides even the most grudging resident the opinion that I am a full citizen of Chancebury in body, loyalty, and emotional connection."

"But with your stepdaughter gone, this is your chance to start over. Elsewhere. Fresh and new."

The simple notion of it made her shake her head vehemently. The action made her think of another "fresh and new" beginning, instituted after Stephen died. "If I left, what of my pies?" she asked. "People have grown to depend on them."

"People depend on meat and milk and even a pint of ale. They do not depend on pies."

"You offend me."

"I mean no offense. I simply speak facts, Esther. If you shutter your pie shop, the world would not shudder."

She stopped their progress to face him. "You offend me again."

He studied her face a moment, then offered her a bow. "Forgive me. I merely want you to be happy. Losing Stephen, bringing up Petunia on your own, then having her leave. . ."

She took his arm and they resumed their walk. "I appreciate your kind hopes. But what you are not considering is how important the pies are to *me*. The shop saved me these past six years. Beyond earning a living, the pies gave me a purpose. The shop is more than something to do, it is something to be."

"I misspoke." He patted her hand. "I have tasted your pies. There are none to rival them."

She had a new thought that might make her point. "Did the eating of my pies make you happy?"

He nodded. "And quite content."

"The baking of those pies has the same effect on me, Clarence. They make me happy and content. Therefore, I will not give them up and risk some possible betterment of life elsewhere for what is already good right here."

"Your point is duly taken."

Finally.

They reached the garden gate of her cottage. "Would you like to come in for some tea?"

"Do you desire the company?"

She considered this a moment. "Actually, I am quite done in."

"Then I will be on my way. Sarah will not sleep well until I am snoring beside her."

Esther kissed his cheek. "Tell her I hope she feels better soon."

"I will." He turned to leave, then stopped. "Remember, Esther. We are always here for you."

"I know, and I thank you for it. Good evening, Clarence, and safe travel home."

He tipped his hat and walked back to the church where his carriage waited.

Esther closed the garden gate and took a moment to look upon her home. For the first time in her life she would live here alone. No Stephen. And now, no Petunia.

Just me.

The day had brought a crucial change that could not be undone. From this moment forward, everything would be different.

She paused to let the thought settle, for surely such a monumental change demanded a monumental response. She took a breath in and let it out, willing for despair or regret to fall upon her and demand release.

Suddenly, another emotion stepped forward, one that was so foreign yet so insistent it would not be denied.

Rather than let its release be public, she quickly stepped inside and latched the door behind her. Assured in her privacy that she would not be the next subject of village gossip, Esther bent her knees low and then jumped into the air, her arms skimming the low ceiling, her shawl flying toward the rungs of the rocking chair.

She landed awkwardly but without a turn of her ankle, and celebrated by laughing aloud at her folly. She covered her mouth, but her joy caused her hand to fall away. Surrendering to the fullness of the moment, she raised her arms above her head and called out, "I am free!"

A giggle followed, and then a waltz among the furniture. She held the skirt of her dress, allowing a porcelain figurine of a shepherd full view of her ankles.

She offered him a curtsy then giggled as if she were a girl of seventeen and not a widow of forty-one.

She retrieved her shawl and hung it on the back of the chair. But another shawl lay where it shouldn't. She plucked Petunia's weekday shawl from a heap at the bottom of the stairs and gathered a pair of her shoes from the edge of the rug. In truth these cast-offs were hers now, as Petunia had told Esther she could have them "as a gift."

Upon closer inspection, Esther found a tear in the shawl and holes in the soles of the shoes.

She shook her head at their condition but knew she shouldn't have expected more. "I've been living with Petunia's cast-offs for a long while now."

Since Stephen's passing to be exact.

His untimely death from falling off a horse represented not just the loss of a husband. His death had meant there would be no more babies for Esther. The two she had carried had not lived, so with Stephen's death, so died the chance of a miracle. Coming to terms with that awful fact she'd thanked God she had Petunia to help her through her grief. But as the fourteen-year-old girl grew older, her attitude worsened. Without the firm hand of her father, she became demanding, selfish, and disobedient. It was as though Petunia felt the world owed her a wage of happiness that she wasn't willing to work for. Esther had done her best to contain and restrain the girl's temperaments, but had cried herself to sleep on many a night, praying for wisdom, patience, and peace.

In order to win her daughter's favor, and in the hope of helping the two of them overcome their grief, Esther had given in too much, accepting the role of second fiddle in her own home.

But no more!

Esther raised the lid of the wood box and tossed Petunia's discards inside, letting the lid fall with a satisfying *clump*.

She found herself grinning for the second time in a very few minutes. Which made her grin all the more.

Energized by her glee, she got another idea. She moved to her late husband's chair — the only comfortable chair in the front room, the chair Petunia had claimed as her own after her father's death. And then she did something she'd never done before.

She sat in it.

Esther nestled into the cushions and stroked the well-worn arms, a habit of Stephen's when he was deep in thought.

She closed her eyes and sighed. "Oh, Stephen. I miss you so much. I had six years with you, and now six years without you. We didn't have enough time, my love." She smiled at the memory of him, the way he'd wink when he teased her, his smile that made everything right, and his loving touch that made the world go away.

"What now, darling?" she whispered.

She didn't expect an answer — certainly not from Stephen. Yet she hoped God heard her plea and would answer her, if not in regard to the moment, in regard to the long run.

Esther took a deep breath of the here and now and looked at her basket of knitting, at the shawl she'd been making for a friend's birthday. Then her eyes strayed to another pastime that remained unfinished. She retrieved a book she had been trying to read for weeks. Perhaps now she would finish it. Perhaps now, in the silence of her cottage, she would read all the books waiting for her on the bookshelf.

She had just found her place when there was a knock at the door.

Perhaps God is answering my "what now" question?

Or else John was returning Petunia, having already had his fill of her.

Esther opened the door and found Chester Mayfield, hat in hand.

"Evening, Esther."

"Chester."

"It was a fine wedding."

"Thank you." At the lag in the conversation, she knew he expected to be asked inside, but she held her ground.

"I. . .I was just checking on you, to see how you be."

"I am fine. Thank you." *Now go on with you.*

He made his hat go full circle in his hands. "Well then."

"Thank you for stopping by," she said.

His double chin turned to triple, but he nodded. "I will see you tomorrow then?"

"I will be at the shop. You may pick up your daily pie, as usual."

She closed the door on him, suffering a twinge of guilt.

But only a twinge. She would not let anything taint this first night of freedom.

Back to her book. But first, she decided to make herself a cup of tea.

With two sugars.

Chapter Two

Esther knocked on the bedroom door. "Petunia, it's time to get up." She waited to hear the familiar groan that indicated Petunia had heard.

There was no groan.

It took Esther a good five seconds to remember the reason for the silence.

Petunia wasn't there. Petunia was married. Esther was alone.

Neither revelation upset her.

She chuckled at her mistake and went downstairs for breakfast. It was then she discovered something else that was different: she didn't need to start the fire. Since the house would remain empty all day — until she came home that evening — there was no need for the added work or the added expense.

She had tea in the pot leftover from last evening and found it quite agreeable to drink cold. She deliberately took out one cup and saucer. One spoon. And one scone from the batch she made last Friday.

The scones would certainly go farther now that Petunia wasn't there to gobble up two each morning. Or three. Her appetites were John's problem now.

In further recognition of her freedom, Esther grabbed her shawl and left the house. She'd eat the scone on the way to the shop.

Despite being earlier than usual, she was not the first to arrive. That chore went to her faithful helper, Sadie Morrow. It was Sadie's job to start the fire in the beehive oven each morning, a task that was begun a good hour before Esther usually arrived, its proper heat not attained until at least an hour after.

When Esther entered the Horton Pie Shop, she found Sadie in the back, sitting near the stove, a pile of wood at the ready to add to the already blazing fire. She held a book in her hands.

She looked up. "Is it that late?" Sadie set the book down and moved to add more wood.

"Calm yourself. It's not late at all," Esther said. "I am simply an hour early." She pointed to the book. "Sit and do as you do every day before I come in. Do not let me disrupt your routine."

With a glance and poke into the oven, Sadie returned to her chair.

"I am happy to see you reading," Esther said. She'd taught Sadie how to read.

Sadie retrieved the book. "I am *trying* to read more than actually reading. I still can't untangle some of the words."

"Show me one that makes you stumble."

Sadie perused a page and pointed to *acrimony*. "Ache-*rim*-on-ee?"

"*A*-cri-mo-nee."

Sadie studied the word a moment, then said, "Pronounced or not, I don't know what it is."

"It means being spiteful or bitter about something."

"Ah." She set the book spread-open on her lap. "Is the house peaceful with Petunia gone?"

That the definition of *acrimony* led to the question was telling. "It is."

"Quiet too, I imagine."

"Quiet too."

Sadie nodded. "I'm happy for you."

"It's traditional to be happy for the bride."

She shrugged. "We both know Petunia will keep happiness at arm's length, just to have something to complain about."

If the statement had been made by another, Esther might have taken offense and come to Petunia's defense. But whether right or wrong, wise or foolish, Sadie knew much about Esther's life, being a willing ear whenever Esther needed to purge her emotions rather than die of them.

"Are you lonely yet?" Sadie asked.

"Not yet." Then she thought of something. "You live alone. Are you lonely?"

"At times it scrapes me from the inside out."

Esther was taken aback. "I am ashamed I didn't know that."

"'Tis nothing unexpected. A woman of thirty-six who's not been wed is used to loneliness sitting by her side. You were lucky. You had a man. And a daughter — such as she was."

Esther said a silent prayer of contrition. "I apologize for not knowing about your struggles. It is apparent that over the years I have done most of the talking and you have done most of the listening."

With a glance to the oven, Sadie added more wood, pushing it in deeper with a hoe. "My life is of little interest. I always enjoy listening to details of yours, for it adds spice to mine. You're going to dinner at the Woodsons' tonight, yes?"

"I am."

"See? Far more excitement than mine." They heard commotion out front. "That will be Fergus with the meat delivery," Sadie said.

"I'll tend to him." Esther vowed to do a better job of tending to Sadie too. It was time to give as much as she'd taken.

**

The hours flew by, as they did every morning. The first pies were already in the oven, and Esther crimped the edges of the next batch, made of mutton.

With a single rap on the door, Chester slipped into the shop.

"We're not open yet, Chester," Esther said. "You know that."

"I do. But I want to order a pie."

Esther had to smile. "Your pie is already in the oven."

"Not the usual meat pie. A different kind. And not for today. For Thursday."

Esther looked up from her work. "What's happening Thursday?"

"You're coming to dinner."

"I am?"

"Will you?"

They had never dined together at his home. The thought of it made her stomach dance a leery dance. She had felt comfortable occasionally sharing a meal at her own house, mainly because Petunia was always present. But to be completely alone with him. . .

She was being silly. They'd known each other for years. He was a good man. "I suppose I could."

"Good," he said with relief. "So make me a special pie on Thursday."

"What kind?"

"Apple."

"You don't like apple pie," Esther said. "Too sweet."

He focused on Esther. "But you like it. It's *your* favorite. Come now, Esther. Dine with me."

She deemed her nerves silly. "Do you cook?"

"I make a mighty stew. I'll buy some bread from the baker's, and with your pie we shall have a fine meal."

She could think of no reason to say no. "I'd be happy to come."

His chubby face lit up as if a light shined from within. "See you at half past seven on Thursday." He glanced toward the back. "I'll come later for me pork pie." With a smile and a nod he left her.

Sadie came into the front of the shop. "You're going to his house for dinner?"

"You shouldn't eavesdrop."

"A woman can't help hearing what a woman can't help hearing."

Esther looked at the door and sighed.

"What's the sigh for?"

She hadn't realized her sigh spoke so loudly. "He's on the press now. Full out."

"The press?"

"Now that Petunia's gone he'll want us to marry."

"Oh."

Esther went back to crimping the pie. "For the past six years, when my 'no thank-yous' fell on deaf ears, I kept his attention at bay with the promise that once Petunia was gone I would be ready."

"Are you?"

"I thought I'd be. But. . ."

Sadie waved an arm toward the door. "If you don't love him, tell him so. Don't be cruel and leave him hanging, more than. . ."

"More than I already have?"

"Six years is a long time for any man to wait."

**

The door to the Woodson home was opened by their twins. "Mama made potatoes with butter," April said.

"Lots of them," May added.

"Do you like buttery potatoes?" Esther asked.

Both eight-year-olds nodded. "We'll eat yours if you don't want 'em."

"You will do no such thing." Their mother, Anne, shooed them away. "Come in, Esther." She jostled little Joe on her hip.

"Chee!" he said, pointing at Esther.

She took his plump little hand and kissed it. "What does 'chee' mean?"

"We have no idea." Anne handed him off. "Will you? I need to check the chicken on the fire."

Esther loved the feel of a young one in her arms, but it was short-lived, as Joe wiggled his way to freedom. He ran to his father's lap as Alexander sat by the fire with his pipe.

"Evening, Esther," the man said. "Have a seat."

"A good evening to you," she said, sitting in the chair opposite. "Thank you for having me."

"Anne was afeared you'd be lonesome in your empty house."

She didn't answer.

"So, are you lonesome?"

"Not yet."

The twins began playing bilbocatch, their voices loudly counting the number of times they caught the ball on the handheld pedestal. Esther expected them to be chastised for their volume, but instead, Alexander set Joe on the floor and took a turn himself to much cheering and applause.

"Twelve!" Alexander said.

"That's not the best, Papa," April said. "I've had fourteen."

"May I try?" Esther asked.

She was handed the toy and twice hit herself with the ball that was attached to the base with a string. "I'm not very good."

"Keep trying," May said.

"Didn't Petunia have one of these?" Alexander asked.

"She did, but she never let me play with it."

Finally, Esther got the ball to land where it should. The room erupted with acclamation, but when she tried for number two, she missed.

"You just need practice," April said.

May darted into a bedroom and came back with a second one. "You can borrow mine to practice at home, if you wish."

"How kind of you, dear." Esther wasn't used to children who willingly shared.

"Dinner is served!" Anne transferred a chicken from a spit on the fire to a serving plate.

They gathered around a table at the other end of the room, with Joe in Anne's lap. Alexander said the blessing, and delicious chicken and very buttery potatoes were served with asparagus and fresh bread.

Esther experienced the dinner as a full participant, but found herself distracted by poignant moments of reflection. The love between the Woodsons was palpable and made Esther remember the good times with her own family. She'd become Petunia's mother when the girl was the same age as the twins. The transition from an unmarried twenty-nine-year-old to a wife and mother had not been easy, but Stephen's love had carried her through.

Did she want to be alone the rest of her life? Or did she wish to be a wife again? A mother?

"You're quiet," Anne said as she wiped Joe's mouth with a corner of her apron.

Esther offered them a grateful smile. "Your joyful home is an inspiration."

Anne exchanged a mischievous smile with her husband. "You don't have to be alone. We all know there is someone who is very willing to make your one two again."

"Has Chester proposed yet?" Alexander asked.

"Darling!" Anne said. "That is too blunt a question."

"One that mirrors your own curiosity, wife."

Anne's cheeks reddened. "With Petunia gone, the entire village is wondering."

"I know."

"So?"

"I am thinking on it."

"You've had six years to think on it, Esther," Anne said. "You are too young and too delightful to be alone."

"I don't plan to be," she said.

Alexander's eyebrows rose. "You have someone else in mind?"

"I don't," she added quickly. "Not specifically."

Anne shook her head. "I cannot think of a single man in Chancebury who might pique your interest."

"Wife, you make the men of the village sound quite abysmal."

"Not abysmal, but they *are* too old, too young, too married, or too. . .tedious."

"Tedious?" Esther asked.

Anne took a moment to think. "Too bashful, boring, brash, boorish, or barbarous."

"Who in Chancebury is barbarous?" Alexander asked.

"Reginald Collins. Have you heard the oaths that come out of his mouth?"

He nodded once. "Agreed."

Esther laughed. "I will admit the male pickings in the village are slim. But does that mean I should settle?"

"Do you think marrying Chester would be settling?" Anne asked.

"No, not at all." *At least I don't think so.*

Anne rose to clear the dishes, and Esther stood to help her. "If you expect some dashing man to ride into town and sweep you off your feet, I'd suggest you

31

toss away the novels you've been reading."

"It could happen," she said.

"When pigs fly," Alexander added.

Esther wouldn't mind seeing a pig fly.

Chapter Three

Thursdays were Esther's favorite day. Any who heard of this preference would find it puzzling, for no one preferred a work day over the freedom from work that Sundays afforded. And why Thursday of all days?

Esther looked forward to Thursday because it wasn't Friday or Saturday when the shop was especially busy with people wanting a pie for Sunday dinner. Or Monday and Wednesday that were also busy with customers wanting a new pie to last them a few days. Tuesday and Thursday were the pie shop's slowest days.

So why Thursday and not Tuesday?

Because Thursday was the day she visited her friend Lady Tomkins. Thursday was the day she could fully be herself.

Each and every Thursday since the pie shop opened, Esther took Verdelia— Verd—two pies—one meat and one sweet. In her economy Verd made the pies last a week, having taught her maidservant to cut them into an exact seven pieces. Esther often wondered what Nelly ate, but since the woman had some heft to her, it was clear she ate well enough when she went home to her husband. Nelly and Sam lived in the caretaker's cottage just a stone's throw from the main house. They were the only servants left at Coventry Hall.

Esther admired Verd for making do. It was difficult to fall from the status of one of the county's elite families to obsolete. From wealth to ruin — or near ruin. For only by Verd's thrift and determination had she been able to stay in the house after her husband's death when the consequences of his gambling debts came to light.

Since then, shame kept Verd in seclusion. Esther was her only friend, her only contact, and though they'd known of each other twelve years, it was only since Stephen's death that their acquaintance had blossomed into friendship.

Esther turned up the driveway leading to the hall. She and Lady

Tomkins first met because Stephen had been the hall's estate manager. His brother, Clarence, and Esther's father had been the solicitors for the baronet and had found Stephen the position when they'd heard Sir Thomas was in need of a manager. That duo had also been instrumental in introducing Esther to Stephen. His wife had died when Petunia was born, and by the time he met Esther, the girl was eight and he had a great desire to finally be a full family. Their marriage and Chancebury had given him his wish.

After the baronet's death—he was shot during a poker game in London—Stephen had helped keep the estate running. But upon Stephen's sudden death a few years later, the hall had slipped into further decay and now was a sad survivor of the once-grand estate. Only then had the widow Lady Tomkins and the widow Esther Horton found the common bond that had lured them into true friendship.

Esther neared the door—that needed a goodly coat of paint. Sam was slacking.

Or perhaps there wasn't money for paint.

She pinched some dead stems from a clump of daisies, then knocked on the door.

Nelly answered. "Good day to you, Mrs. Horton," she said.

"And good day to you, Nelly." She leaned close. "How is she today?"

"*She* is fine," called Verd from the parlor. "How did you think she'd be?"

Esther and Nelly shared a smile, and the pies were handed over for Nelly to take to the kitchen building out back.

Esther entered the parlor and leaned down to kiss her friend's cheek and give her cat, Christopher, a scratch behind the ears. "If I remember correctly, last week you had a headache."

"You didn't think it bad enough to visit me between then and now," Verd said, nodding toward Esther's usual chair that had been drawn close.

"I had a wedding to attend."

Verd blinked twice. "Ah. Yes. So Petunia is finally someone else's problem."

Esther removed her bonnet and set it on a side table. "You are too harsh."

"I only know what you tell me, girl. If I am harsh it is because you have presented her so."

Esther smoothed her skirt over her knees. Only Verd would call Esther a girl. Yet compared to Verd's seventy-some years, age was relative. "Perhaps I *have* been too harsh."

"Perhaps you haven't."

Esther chuckled softly. "Perhaps I haven't."

"There now," Verd said. "At least we have that truth settled. So tell me what else is new in the world of Chancebury."

Esther knew it was best to get to the base of it, especially since Nelly was otherwise-occupied making tea. The fewer ears that heard, the better.

"Chester is taking me at my word — about *after* Petunia leaves home."

"So he hasn't forgotten about you?"

"Not in the least."

Verd stroked the length of Christopher's black coat. He began to purr. "You *are* rather unforgettable."

"You flatter me, Lady Tomkins."

"I only speak the truth."

"It is your greatest gift." Her words were more than flattery. "*That* is the truth."

"My, my, we are replete with compliments today. Yet I long for otherwise."

"You do like the gossip."

Verd spread her arms wide. "These walls have told me all the stories they are going to tell. I depend on you to keep me entertained."

"You could venture out. Come to dinner. Just us two."

"What would I gain by that? I have your company here. I do not need to go elsewhere for it."

"No one in the village blames you for your husband's. . ."

"Nastiness?"

Esther nodded. "It has been a long time. I promise your reentry into the village would be painless."

"But I rarely went to the village before Thomas died. I knew of their suffering under his so-called patronage, for it was my own." The wrinkles on her face multiplied.

The discussion was interrupted by Nelly bringing the tea. The smell of earth and smoke toured the room. Verd poured milk and sugar in both cups, just the way Esther liked, then handed her a cup.

"There now. Chester. Are you enjoying his attention?"

"Partly."

"You have been partly enjoying it for six years. I assume he wants the all of you?"

"He does."

Verd's grey eyebrows rose. "He has proposed?"

"Not yet. Though he has invited me to dinner tonight."

"What are your thoughts on the matter?"

Esther held the cup beneath her chin, letting its aromatic vapors calm her. "I am not certain I wish to marry anyone."

"Ever?"

"That, I don't know. But certainly I hesitate regarding now. I am only forty-one."

"That old?"

"You should talk."

"I agree. There is time for you. But your hesitance involves issues more than age, does it not?"

"Although it is new to me, I think I enjoy having the house to myself."

"That statement is as weak as this tea." Verd set her cup down. "I swear Nelly uses the leaves leftover from her morning pot with Sam."

Esther ignored the complaint. "There is a quote from Cicero that I hold dear."

"Since when do you read Cicero?"

"I have read him off and on. But I've been keeping this quotation in my pocket for when it suited my life."

"And the quotation is. . . ?"

"'I am never less alone than when alone.'"

Verd clapped her hands together. "Aye! That is a good one. Well said."

"I've always thought so." She took a sip of tea. "When Petunia was home I felt glimmers of satisfaction, but never felt it fully until this week when I have the house totally to myself."

Verd nodded. "I understand. I do not mind being alone these seven years. For I have my own good company, yours on occasion, and the Lord's on all occasions. What more do I need?"

"Perhaps your example has inspired me."

She moved her arm so Christopher could jump to the floor. He meandered out of the room and up the grand stairway.

"I enjoyed the love of one good man," Esther said. "I do not need another."

"I did not enjoy the love of one good man, and never found another."

Esther had heard many stories of Verd's husband—from Verd, from Stephen, and from the citizens of Chancebury. A more contrary man had never lived. Sir Thomas held all things in contempt, whether they deserved his judgment or not. He never graced Chancebury with a stroll through the square, but arrived and departed in an enclosed carriage, with not even a wave to mark his passing. The only time anyone saw him was when they fell into his ill graces by not providing perfection of some item or service. His tenants would sell their youngest child to pay the rent on time, for Sir Thomas had never been averse to calling in the law. Which of course had led to eviction or debtor's prison on more than one occasion—in spite of Stephen's best efforts and calls for mercy and understanding. And financial intervention. On more than one occasion, Stephen had paid the debt—without Sir Thomas' knowledge.

It was ironic the baronet had died in debt. It was a bad end to a bad man, who had left a good wife and a spoiled and willful son.

Speaking of. . . "How is your son?"

"According to his rather insufficient letters, Thaddeus thrives on the Continent, having no interest in the hall or the duties of baronet. Or his duties as my son."

"Does he plan a visit soon?"

She flipped the question away with a hand. "He, his wife, and their daughters are busy being busy. They have no time for me."

Their lack of interest saddened Esther. Unfortunately they shared the grief of ungrateful children.

Verd shook her head in a short burst, as though dispelling the subject. "I do have a visit to look forward to."

"Who is coming?"

"My nephew."

"Henry?"

"The same. He comes next week."

"All the way from London?"

She raised a finger. "He is not in London anymore. He recently became the headmaster at a school in Manchester."

"How delightful. He has never been the head before, has he?"

"He has not. He has been a teacher for sixteen years. It is time he rises up. And *he* writes a delightful letter."

"I would like to meet him sometime."

"I am sure that can be arranged."

Esther noticed her smile was slightly wicked.

"Do not match us up, friend," Esther said. "Did I not just say I enjoy my newfound freedom?"

Verd offered an exaggerated sigh. "Alas, you did." She winked. "But you can still meet him." Verd set her teacup down. "Actually, I have something even more important to speak with you about."

"What's that?"

"I have a confession to make."

Esther grinned. "Do tell."

"Nothing scandalous, I assure you. It's rather pitiful, really."

Esther leaned forward and touched her knee. "What's wrong?"

"In spite of our courageous talk, I have been feeling rather lonely of late."

"I am sorry for that. I could come visit more often."

Verd held up a hand. "I appreciate your offer, but at Henry's suggestion I have decided on another remedy."

"You have my attention."

"I have locked myself away for years. You have been my only contact with the village, but now. . . It is time for a change."

"Are you going to town?"

"Pooh. Not that much of a change. But I would like to meet the people of Chancebury. I was thinking it was time to let some people in — people other than you. Are you jealous?"

"Not at all. I think it's wonderful. But how —"

"I wish to invite them here."

It took Esther a moment to comprehend her meaning. "All of them?"

She seemed taken aback. "The village has not grown by that much, has it?"

"I have no knowledge of the actual population, but I would imagine it is close to two hundred, all told."

"Oh dear. That many."

"You could invite a few."

She shook her head. "It will be all or nothing. For I turn eighty on the second of next month."

Less than two weeks from now. "I congratulate you, but to arrange a party so quickly. . ."

"A person only turns eighty once, and such a milestone deserves a mighty celebration. And so I say, let them come — at least let all be invited." She pointed to her desk. "Fetch the paper there, noting the details."

Esther found the piece of paper in question, which listed foods to be served.

"Add your pies to the list."

"Of course."

"Do you think people will come?"

Esther chuckled. "They will. For you and this house have been the subject of their curiosity for years."

"Ha," Verd said with a grin. "I do like keeping them in suspense."

Esther looked at the information. "How do you propose to spread the word?"

"I thought you could post a sign at your shop and on the windows of a few other shops in the village. And perhaps Pastor Wilkins could mention it next Sunday?"

"Would you like help making the notices?"

Verd nodded toward the desk. "I have pen and paper right there. How many do you think we shall need?"

**

Back in the shop, it was time to close up and go to dinner at Chester's. Esther draped her shawl over her shoulders and tied it with a knot, needing her hands for the apple pie.

"Shouldn't you go home and put on a nicer dress?" Sadie asked. "Eating at Chester's is a special occasion."

Esther glanced down at the blue-sprigged dress she'd worn the entire day. Although she'd worn an apron, she could see flour on the skirt. She brushed it off and made a decision. "I should, but I'm not going to. I don't want to encourage him by dressing up."

"Don't you think going to dinner will encourage him?"

Esther gave the shawl's knot an extra tug. "Maybe I shouldn't go."

"Maybe you shouldn't."

Sadie's words made Esther look at her. "You think so?"

Sadie wrapped her own shawl close and headed to the door. "Just go. You need to eat."

Esther nodded and took up the pie.

"Be nice to him," Sadie said as she closed the door behind them. "Chester deserves that."

**

Esther had walked past Chester's cottage a thousand times before this evening. It was near his smithy, though sufficient steps away to escape the smoke and cinders.

She could see firelight through the window. Her thought of *he's in there* was absurd. Of course he was in there. She approached the door.

"Good evening, Esther," came a familiar woman's voice.

Esther turned around and saw Myrtle Cray strolling by. "Evening, Myrtle."

"Say hello to Chester for me," she said with a smile as she passed.

Esther faced the door again, hating that of all people to see her at Chester's, it was the town gossip. Myrtle was a fly in the peaceful ointment of Chancebury. She buzzed from this to that, listening in, seeing what she shouldn't, and annoying people until they wanted to swat her away. She was as small in mind as she was in stature.

The door opened. "I thought I heard someone out here."

"It's just me." *More absurdity. Esther, gather your wits!*

He stepped aside. "Come in."

She entered a cottage that was ablaze with a cozy fire and a lit candle on the small table—which was set with two pewter bowls, plates, and spoons. In the center of the table was a tankard filled with wildflowers.

"How prettily done, Chester."

"I wanted to make it nice. Since we're having stew, I wasn't sure we needed the plates, but then I thought of the bread and pie and—" He noticed her holding it and took it from her.

"You did a fine job of the setting," she said.

He let out a breath. It was then she noticed he had also done a fine job in regards to his own appearance. He wore his Sunday vest, and his hair was slicked back from its usual tousle.

"Is that pomade in your hair?" she asked.

He moved to touch it, but stopped short. "Anne at the mercantile sold it to me. I thought I would give a go of it. It's silly but—"

"You look very nice," she said. And she wasn't lying. Not really. Although Chester could never be considered handsome and was a bit more portly than most, his countenance was agreeable enough. His smile made up for any lack in his looks.

At this point she felt badly for not going home to change clothes. "I feel underdressed."

"You look beautiful," he said, "as always."

She felt herself blush but didn't need to worry about him seeing it, as he moved to stir the stew on the fire.

"It smells delicious."

"There's not much to go wrong with meat and vegetables." He moved the wrought-iron cooking crane aside so it was away from direct heat. "It appears ready. Shall we?" He motioned to the table then held her chair.

He took the bowls to the pot and ladled a goodly portion. Then he sliced the bread and offered her a piece.

"Here's some of Mrs. Cooley's blackberry jam, and the stew may need some salt." He pushed a wooden salt cellar toward her. "But you might taste it first."

He began to pick up his spoon, but stopped when he saw her bow her head.

"Oh. Sorry. I's out of the habit."

At his request, she said a blessing, and the meal commenced. Blessedly the conversation centered around town news. Mr. Parker bought a new horse. Mrs. Donnelly had a fifth child — another boy. And the Wilsons were expecting his cousins from London for a visit. Esther told him about Lady Tomkins' birthday celebration. When they spoke of Petunia's wedding, Esther feared Chester would bring up her vow to marry him.

He didn't mention it.

As they ate the last bites of the apple pie — which of course, was delicious — Esther could finally breathe freely. She'd made it through the dinner without talking about their relationship.

Chester pushed his empty plate away and sat back, groaning with contentment. "I am full to overflowing."

Although his words could be construed in an indelicate way, Esther agreed. "It was a delicious meal. Thank you for inviting me." She heard the clock strike nine and began to stand. "I must get home. The mornings come early for both of us."

He helped with her chair, but as she stepped aside, he took her hand in both of his, their large size engulfing hers. "Esther."

With that one word, she knew what was coming.

She wanted to flee, but smiled as much as she could manage and gently pulled her hand free. "Again, thank you for your kind hospitality."

His face contorted with panic, and he took her hand again. "Esther. It's time."

No, it isn't!

Before she could stop him, he got down on one knee — with a groan — and gazed up at her. "Esther Horton, I love you. Will you be my wife?"

A thousand words sped through her mind, and she feared she wouldn't find the right ones. But then she said, "I will think about it."

He looked confused, then smiled and rose to standing. "It is a more positive answer than, 'no thank you.'"

She smiled back. "I believe it is."

"Let me walk you home."

She glanced outside and saw that the summer sun had not fully set. "I will be all right," she said. "I will see you tomorrow for your Friday pie?"

"You will."

On impulse, she kissed him on the cheek and left. She did more than leave, she fled like a released prisoner fearing the jailer would change his mind.

Esther felt dreadful for her attitude. She'd just received a proposal from a very nice man, and as the Woodsons had pointed out, one of the only eligible men in Chancebury. He was also a very patient man. She should be flying down the road on the wings of love.

Wings of like. For I do like him.

But it was not enough. Not nearly enough.

Chapter Four

And they all said, "Amen."

Esther sat next to Sadie in their usual pew. Everyone in Chancebury had their spots, which made it easy for the pastor to see who had found something else to do with their Sunday mornings. In the days following Sunday, Pastor Wilkins made it a habit to check on each absentee. Those who had good reason—their death bed—would be comforted. Those who slept late or decided the morning too perfect for fishing would receive Pastor Wilkins's rebuke. And if repeatedly tested, there were opportunities to weed the cemetery or scrape candle wax from the sanctuary floor and altar.

The possibility of the pastor's reprimand had no bearing on Esther's loyal attendance. In actuality, his sermons were not the draw, either. What did draw her to her self-appointed place was her need for peace. Apart from the busyness of everyday life and the drama that spun around Petunia and Chester, church allowed Esther the chance to close her eyes, fully invite God in, and banish the world. At least for a little while.

Her head bowed, she half-listened to the pastor's prayer—which leaned toward verbosity and lofty language meant to impress. She could not be certain, but since Jesus came to earth in such a humble manner, and since all accounts of His life featured His love and concern for His flock devoid of self-aggrandizement, Esther had long ago chosen to drown out Pastor Wilkins's drone of a prayer in preference for her own simple entreaties to the Lord. Gratitude, hallelujahs, and cries for help wove together into a durable, threefold cord.

She was just bringing the subject of Chester before the Almighty, when she heard him—Chester, not the Lord—clear his throat in the pew behind her.

There he is, Lord. What do I do with Chester? Are we to be together? Should I remain alone? Or is there someone. . . ?

The congregation stood to sing a hymn, forcing Esther to leave go of her prayer. She shared a hymnal with Sadie and sang:

"Give me a new, a perfect heart,
From doubt, and fear, and sorrow free;
The mind which was in Christ impart,
And let my spirit cleave to Thee."

She smiled as she sang, for as often happened, the words suited her state of mind, as if God Himself had chosen the hymn just for her.

Chester's mellow baritone rang out behind her, causing her to share a smile with Sadie.

"'Cause me to walk in Christ my Way,'" he sang, *"'and I Thy statutes shall fulfill. In every point Thy law obey, and perfectly perform Thy wi-ll-ll.'"*

By holding out the last note — beyond every other voice in the sanctuary — Esther knew Chester wanted her to turn around and smile at him. Although she knew she shouldn't, she couldn't help herself.

He gave her a smile in return. And a wink. Somehow the wink seemed a bit cheeky for the house of God, so she quickly faced forward.

Cheeky or not, Chester made her think happy thoughts.

Had God answered her prayer already?

**

The congregation exited the church, taking turns shaking Pastor Wilkins's hand. Esther welcomed the chance to thank him for mentioning Verd's eightieth birthday party on September sixteenth.

At the bottom of the steps, Esther spotted a mighty contingent of Chancebury's finest gossips.

"Good morning, Esther," Myrtle Cray said. "Chester."

"Do you two have plans for the rest of the day?" another asked.

Another looked to the sky. "'Tis a fine summer day."

Chester touched Esther's arm. "Indeed it is. Mrs. Horton, would you care for a walk?"

In an instant Esther knew that rejecting him would cause more unwanted gossip than agreeing. "If you'd like."

Chester offered his arm, and together they walked away from the church.

"They were lying in wait for us," she said. "Ready to pounce."

"I don't object to their suggestion. Do you?"

"I object to their assumption."

"Ah." He nodded once. "'Tis not a horrible assumption, is it?"

She sighed. She was making a mess of things. "Not at all. Forgive me. I simply object to having any part of my life be a foregone conclusion."

He laughed. "Like Myrtle being a gossip and the boredom of Pastor's sermons?"

She had to laugh with him. "I find both of interest—on occasion."

"Not often enough." He pointed toward the sky. "God is up there and we are down here. When I die I want to be up there, too. Beyond that, I don't need a pastor spouting off shalt-nots at me."

"That's a rather simplistic notion of faith."

He shrugged. "I am a simple man."

"But what about trying to deepen your faith? What about the power of prayer? What about somehow discovering why we are here, now?"

He shook his head and pointed at a path that led from the main road into the meadow and woods beyond. "Shall we?"

Esther mourned his lack of interest in discussing anything profound. Their conversations were always amiable but occasionally she would have liked to discuss subjects beyond the moment.

"Come on," he said, pulling her toward the path.

She glanced behind and saw the other churchgoers walking home, including Myrtle and her cronies. "I think it best we stay on the road."

Chester glanced back, too. "Perhaps I should shock the lot of them by gathering you in my arms and leaning you into a low dip."

She swatted his arm and let go. "You will do no such thing."

"I will not. But it is pleasurable to think about."

Actually, it was.

**

Although Esther knew the Sabbath was supposed to be a day of rest, once home from church her thoughts whirled in such a frenzied fashion that she failed all seemly Sunday pursuits such as reading a book, praying over the Bible, or knitting. She was spurred into bodily action lest she burst — which would be the essence of unseemly.

She retrieved a basket and went to her garden — her pride and joy. Stephen's pride and joy. She hadn't shown much interest in it until he passed, but then she discovered it held much satisfaction. It was also highly integral to her livelihood. For without the vegetables and fruits from said garden, her pies would bring less profit. She already had to purchase the meats for the filling. And the flour and sugar. And butter and eggs. To self-provide the other filling ingredients was a godsend.

She strolled through the rows and gathered ripe berries. That an occasional berry never made it to the basket was payment for her work. But bending down so long made her back ache, and she stood and arched it with a groan.

"No rest for the weary?"

She looked over her shoulder and saw Chester standing on the road, a bouquet of flowers in his hands. "It appears you've been doing your own picking."

He walked to the low fence that formed an edge between them and held them out to her. "I meant to get you some flowers this morning on our walk. You can blame Myrtle Cray for the delay."

She left her basket on the ground and stepped over a row of berry plants to take the white flowers. "Thank you."

"They are forget-me-nots."

"I think not. They are fool's parsley."

"No! They are forget-me-nots."

"I appreciate the sentiment, but as it is August, forget-me-nots are past. You hold fool's parsley."

His countenance fell and she felt badly for being too specific. "Whatever they are called I thank you for your effort."

"I considered bringing you some Bachelor Buttons, but I didn't want to be associated with such a flower anymore, and so. . ."

She held the flowers to her nose, but disliked the scent. "Thank you, Chester."

He nodded. Sighed. Then looked to the fruit trees. "You have apples that need picking."

"I was going to get the Tanner boy to help me."

"No need. I am here. Where is your ladder?"

"Remember it's the Sabbath, Chester. I don't want to lure you into sin by making you work."

"I heard Pastor say something about the harvest being plenteous, but the laborers few."

"So you were listening."

"Occasionally."

"I believe he was referring to harvesting souls, not apples."

He paused but a moment. "Your pies are a harvest to my soul, Esther."

She wasn't sure if it was an apt analogy, but again appreciated his effort. She pointed to the ladder on the side of the house.

**

As she got into bed that night, Esther found herself smiling and knew there was only one reason.

His name was Chester Mayfield.

They'd had a very enjoyable afternoon picking apples and a very enjoyable evening eating a simple dinner of bread, cheese, and chopped apples mixed with cinnamon and sugar.

"I am far satisfied," she told the bedroom as she blew out the candle.

The smell of burnt tallow wafted over her, encircling her words.

She sat up in bed. "*Am* I far satisfied? If so, it is Chester's doing." She thought of her prayer that morning when she'd asked God if He wanted her to be with Chester.

And then Chester had shown up with flowers and an eager spirit.

Esther looked heavenward. "It's him, isn't it, Lord? You want me to be with Chester."

She snuggled into the cozy comfort of her bed and let God's answer tuck her in.

Chapter Five

Chester beamed as he came into the pie shop. "Good afternoon, ladies. Are you ready for the September Festival?"

Esther looked to Sadie, and the two women nodded. "Fifteen pies ready to sell by the slice," Esther said. "Help us get a few of them to the table outside. People are already gathering in the square."

With Chester's help, half the pies were transferred, as were a mish-mosh of plates and forks that Esther had gathered over the years for just such an occasion. She placed small notes next to each pie to mark the selection: lamb, beef, apple, raspberry, cherry, and even trout— caught by Chester in the river.

He adjusted the bench behind the table. "Will this suit you, Sadie?"

"It does. Thank you, Chester."

Was Sadie blushing?

Esther didn't have time to ponder the question, as their first customer arrived. "Mr. Bowens, how can I tempt you today?"

**

The music was infectious.

Chester approached and held out his hand. "Shall we?"

Esther glanced at the table.

"There are only five slices left," he said. "I'll buy them all myself if it will get you to dance with me."

"Go on," Sadie said from her place nearby. "Dance."

Esther was drawn into the crowd of revelers and let the music of the fiddle, pipe, and drum transport her to a place of pure pleasure and merriment. Those who weren't dancing offered their encouragement by clapping in time — and hooting when the music gave special delight.

One dance led to the next, and Esther felt a catch in her side. She begged off the next song then saw Sadie, standing forlorn. "Chester, go ask Sadie to dance."

He looked in her direction, nodded, then added, "But only because you look done in."

She waved him off and moved to the bench. Chester stood before Sadie and bowed like a gallant. "Miss Morrow? May I have the pleasure?"

Sadie looked to Esther for permission. "Please," Esther said with a wave. "Wear him out."

Sadie looked absolutely gleeful as Chester whirled her around.

Myrtle approached and handed Esther a folded fan. "It appears you need this more than I."

She accepted the offer. The breeze of the fan refreshed in spite of the foul wind of its owner. "Chester is quite indefatigable."

"He is indeed tireless." Myrtle smiled. "And persistent, I would guess?"

Luckily, Esther's face was already reddened.

"Come now, Esther," Myrtle said. "Everyone in Chancebury is waiting for Chester and Esther to tie the knot. For with those two names, how can you not? Has he not asked?"

"Mostly," she said.

"What an odd way to put it."

I've said too much already.

"So if he has mostly asked, what did you mostly say?"

"I said I would think about it."

"And have you?"

"Very much."

Myrtle tossed her pudgy hands in the air. "Then what say you, woman? Give the poor man an answer or set him free."

Esther was shocked by her choice of words. "He is free already."

"He most certainly is not. He has set his cap on you and you alone. You're not being fair, Esther Horton. Nor even polite."

Esther hated being lectured about courtesy by the likes of Myrtle Cray. To put an end to the conversation, she handed the fan back. Luckily, the song also ended, and she saw Chester turning in her direction with a glowing Sadie by his side.

Myrtle leaned close. "Give him your answer this very day—before you lose him."

Lose him?

She watched Chester and Sadie chat happily as they came closer.

Sadie?

And Chester?

She had not seen any attraction between them.

Or had she?

They reached the table.

"Thank you for the dance, Chester," Sadie said. "You are a fine dancer."

"As are you, Miss Morrow." He turned to Myrtle. "I may have to borrow your fan."

She handed it to him, and he let himself look silly with its use.

"Why don't you and Esther take a walk?" Myrtle said. "Find a nice breeze along the lane."

He looked confused—as was Esther, until she received the busybody's pointed look.

Oh. Yes. That.

Chester returned the fan then offered Esther his arm. "I will never reject a stroll with my Esther."

My Esther.

Although she hated being propelled to action by Myrtle, with a glance to Sadie—who looked troubled—Esther took his arm and together they walked away from the square.

She was suddenly tongue-tied. Had the time actually come for her to answer Chester's proposal?

He noticed her silence. "You are quiet. And your face melancholy. Is something troubling you? I only asked Sadie to dance because you asked me to."

She shook her head. "That's not it. I *did* ask you to."

"Then what is it?"

She waited until some children ran by then stopped to face him. "Ask me the question you asked in your cottage."

He blinked, then smiled. "Really?"

She suffered a wave of panic and could only nod.

He took her hands in his. "Esther, will you marry me?"

Although she knew she should say yes with enthusiasm, she found she couldn't respond without full honesty. "I don't want to say yes, but can think of no reason to say no."

"Good enough!" He drew her into his arms and kissed her on the lips.

"Kissy-missy!" a boy called out.

"Oooh," said another.

The couple separated, but Chester kept his arm around her. "Be nice, boys, and perhaps you too can win the hand of a good woman someday."

"Yer getting' married?"

"We are."

The boys ran toward the square, shouting the news. "Mr. Mayfield and Mrs. Horton are getting hitched!"

To have the entire village know in such quick fashion overwhelmed. Yet what did Esther expect?

Chester kissed her forehead. "Shall we go accept their congratulations?"

Esther didn't want to say yes, but could think of no reason to say no.

Chapter Six

I am betrothed.

Esther lay in bed the morning after saying yes to Chester and let the thought settle.

She did not smile. She did not frown.

A white butterfly entered her room with the morning breeze, fluttered about, then escaped outside again. Carefree. Without responsibilities or consequences to weigh it down.

Being betrothed was all about responsibilities and consequences, but it was also about joy and anticipation. Oddly she felt little of anything. She was lukewarm. Neither hot nor cold. It was not a pleasant sensation.

God does not like lukewarm. She remembered a verse and repeated it aloud. "'Because thou art lukewarm, and neither cold nor hot, I will spue thee out of my mouth.'"

That this nothingness of feeling left her joyless *and* disgusted the Almighty, meant something had to be done about it.

But what?

To clear her head, she felt the need to talk it through with someone. She dressed quickly and walked toward the church — toward the cemetery where Stephen was buried. Stephen would know what to do. She knew the thought ridiculous but still hoped talking to him — hearing her words said aloud in the coolness of the cloudy day would nudge her one way or the other.

It looked like rain. But if she hurried. . .

As she passed the path that she and Chester were going to take into the meadow the previous Sunday, she turned upon it to gather some wildflowers for Stephen's grave. She chose asters and bachelor buttons — the latter making her smile.

As she retraced her steps toward the road, she heard a carriage coming. Just as she paused to let it pass, an awful racket sounded as the wheel of the carriage cracked. The cabriolet tilted precariously to its side on half a wheel. The horse dragged it a few feet, nearly losing its footing, forcing spokes to pop and splinter.

Esther ran to help.

When the carriage fully halted, she saw that a man had fallen toward the lower side of the chaise, an awkward leg extended outward for balance.

Esther tossed the flowers aside. "Sir! Are you all right?"

He glanced at her while pushing himself away from the tilt, with effort gaining his feet upon the ground. He staggered a few steps and took a deep breath, straightened his clothing then assessing the damage. "I appear to be in one piece. Thank God."

"I thank Him, too," Esther said. "It could have been far worse."

He put his hat to his chest and looked heavenward. "Again, I thank You, Lord."

Esther had her first free moment to give him her full attention. She was impressed. He was very tall and had tousled hair the color of wheat. He was dressed beautifully in buff trousers, a blue weskit, and a dark cutaway coat covered with a black cloak.

"Now that the dust has cleared. . . Madam," he said with a bow.

"Sir." Esther bobbed a curtsy and found her heart flutter. How unusual.

He returned his hat to his head and smiled at her. It was not an ordinary smile, but it seemed to signal the completion of a pleasurable transaction, as if one plus one equaled. . .

"Are you here to save me?" he asked.

She smiled. "Perhaps."

He helped her negotiate the tall grass at the edge of the road so they could speak in closer proximity.

She pointed at the wheel. "There is a wainwright in town. You should ask for Mr. Mayfield."

Just as the information was exchanged, she felt a raindrop. And then another.

The heavens opened.

"Come!" He removed his cloak and held it as a shield over Esther as he helped her into the tilted chaise. He quickly pulled the leather roof over them. Together they held the cloak over the front opening, creating further protection.

The rain pelted. Thunder rumbled.

She could smell coffee upon his breath.

"Well then," he said. "That was unexpected."

She saw him press his feet against the floorboard as he tried to keep a respectable distance.

"I apologize," he said. "Tight quarters."

"It cannot be helped." And actually, she didn't mind his closeness. For he had fascinating eyes, as pale as a foggy sky. She wished it were possible to see them in full light. To stare at them.

Stop it, Esther. You're acting like a lovesick girl.

"You say the name of the wainwright is Mayfield?"

"Chester Mayfield," she said. Then she noticed his hand was bleeding. "You cut yourself."

He couldn't inspect his hand without compromising their shelter. "It appears I did. It's nothing that won't heal."

"As I said, it could have been far worse. If the horse hadn't stopped, you could have been flung out."

"A broken wheel can be mended."

"Far easier than broken bones."

Suddenly there was silence. The rain stopped as abruptly as it began. "Well then," he said.

Esther endured a wave of disappointment, as though she'd been told there would be no Christmas.

"Here. Let me take the cloak for both of us." He took over her handhold of it, and their fingers touched. His lingered mere seconds, yet with that brief contact, Esther felt like she'd enjoyed a full caress. How utterly odd. And magnificent.

He tilted the cloak outward, then quickly swept it to the far side amid a flurry of droplets that spattered the back of the horse.

They sat in the carriage a moment, confirming the obvious. Since the rain had stopped, regrettably, their need to sit close was over.

"Let me get out, and then I will help you." He stepped to the ground then extended his hand toward Esther. She welcomed the chance to touch him again.

But there was more.

Due to the precariousness of the tilt, he took hold beneath her arms and lifted her to the ground.

Don't let go! met with *Why am I responding this way?*

His hands moved to her upper arms for a fleeting moment. "Are you all right?"

"Not even damp, thanks to you."

He swept his top hat into a bow. "I thank you for your company, milady. I. . .I guess I will be on my way."

"You are welcome, sir." With a curtsy she reluctantly turned in the opposite direction of the village and walked toward the church. She enjoyed an uncommon spring to her step. She should not be smiling, for there had been a carriage accident. A broken wheel. A close call to dire injury.

The source of her smile belonged to the man.

Then —

"I don't know his name!"

She stopped in the road, looked back, and saw him rounding a curve. At that moment he also looked back. And waved.

Esther waved, too. At the man. Without a name.

"Why didn't we exchange names? We spoke of the rain and the wheel, but not our names? What is wrong with me?" She remembered her lukewarm emotions that morning. Her current feelings were far from lukewarm. But for the wrong reasons.

Her need to talk to Stephen increased.

She continued her walk to the cemetery and to his headstone. She regretted tossing her flowers away but knew Stephen would forgive her. She would have knelt but for the wet grass. Instead she stood, faced the stone, and sighed deeply. "Oh, Stephen." She wasn't sure what to say next, so settled for the obvious. "I miss you. And I'm so confused." She continued with her confession. "I am engaged to Chester, but I feel little for the fact, as though I am numb or uncaring. I shouldn't be uncaring about such a happy event, should I?"

She peered back toward the road, her memories returning to the man in the carriage.

"I met another man today, Stephen. I know nothing of him but for a feeling of immediate connection. I remember feeling such a way when I met you, how the hint of your touch would course through me as though I were on fire." She shook her head and plucked a weed from the grass. "'Tis silly. Completely and entirely. I don't even know his name."

She heard movement behind her. Her heart leapt. *He's come back!*

But it wasn't the man. It was Pastor Wilkins. She forced a smile to cover her disappointment. "Pastor."

"Mrs. Horton. How are you today?"

She nodded toward the headstone. "I am chatting with Stephen."

He smiled. "How is he?"

"Probably very fine, tending to God's garden, but I. . ."

Should she say something?

"Yes?"

"I am not so fine."

He looked surprised. "You are newly engaged to a fine man. I would think your heart would be soaring."

You would think.

"Is your betrothal at issue?"

"No. Not. . .exactly."

"You have been married before, Mrs. Horton. Surely you approve of the institution."

She glanced toward Stephen's grave. "I had a very happy marriage."

"You have known Chester for many years."

"As long as I have been in Chancebury."

"He has been attentive during the years since Stephen died."

She let a nod be her answer.

His brow furrowed. "Do you know of any defect of his character?"

"None. He is a fine man. Of impeccable character."

Pastor Wilkins spread his arms. "There it is then."

She let out a breath. "There it is."

"You have been through much lately, what with Petunia's wedding. Be happy in the change, and look forward not back."

"I am looking forward, I just. . ." There was nothing more to say that he would understand. "It's nothing. I should go. I'm late. Sadie has been all alone at the shop far too long."

He put a hand to his chin. "Perhaps she could man the post a while longer?"

"You have a task for me?"

"An opinion, if you will. About candles." He gestured toward the church. "Shall we?"

**

After long deliberation, a decision regarding the church candles was accomplished. While Esther wished to be anywhere but there, Pastor Wilkins painstakingly detailed the dilemma: should they continue to use the low-light — and ill-smelling — tallow candles which were offered for free by Mrs. Collins who made them out of pig fat from her farm? The alternatives were whale-oil candles for brighter light or the even more expensive beeswax candles. Apparently the alternatives offered a longer life, no bad smell, less mess, and brighter light. But they were not free.

To finish with the matter — and in an attempt to prevent herself from screaming in frustration because Esther didn't care which candles were used and saw no need for her opinion in the first place—she offered to pay for the first lot of whale-oil candles from her proceeds earned during the festival. Only upon leaving did she wonder if that was the pastor's intent all along.

Free at last, she hurried toward the village with new purpose. For halfway into Pastor Wilkins' candle dissertation, she realized the man from the carriage was in Chancebury right that minute. He was at Chester's. If she wanted to see him—and find out his name—she had to hurry and catch him before the wheel was repaired and he was gone from her forever.

She ignored the intimacy and idiocy of the latter phrase, her need to know overriding common sense. A mantra of *please be there, please be there* spurred her to walk so fast her heart raced and a trickle of perspiration tickled down her back.

But then she saw him in the road beside the carriage, assisting Chester as the wheel was replaced. She forced herself to slow down and put a hand to the strands of hair that had escaped her bonnet.

He turned in her direction. And smiled. Esther waved and hurried the last few steps. "I see it is nearly fixed."

"It is," the man said. "Due to your recommendation of Mr. Mayfield."

Chester continued to work. "So you're the woman who helped him?"

"I am."

The man stepped forward. "I believe we parted without being introduced. I am—"

Chester stood and wiped his hands on his thighs. "Mr. Waters, meet Mrs. Horton, my—"

Esther stopped him before the word *fiancée* could be placed in the air between them. "Nice to meet you, Mr. Waters," she said with a curtsy.

"It is a pleasure to properly meet you."

Chester turned toward him. "That will be half a crown."

Mr. Waters produced the payment. "Thank you for your service, sir."

Chester nodded.

"Well then," Mr. Waters said. He paused as though wishing to expand the moment. But it could only be expanded so far. "I will be off. Good day to you both." He climbed into the carriage and, with a tip of his hat, was on his way.

A wave of regret swept over Esther, making her heart heavy and her feet leaden. *Don't go!*

Chester gathered his tools and placed them in his wagon. "You are just going to town?"

"Pastor Wilkins needed my advice."

"Better you giving him advice than the flip of it. Come. I'll drive you to the shop."

Getting into the wagon, Esther realized Chester might be able to help her. "What an interesting man."

"Who?"

"Mr. Waters."

He shrugged. "Just a man. I'm glad for the business. I usually charge two shillings, but thought he could afford the extra."

"That wasn't very nice."

"I was nice enough to go out and get his wheel in the first place, bring it back, then fix it, then go back again to replace it."

He was right. "Where is he from?

Where is he going?"

"What's that to me? Or you?"

She looked to the side of the road so he would not see the flush she felt in her cheeks. "We don't get many strangers through Chancebury. I was just curious. You spent much time with him."

"I spent little time *with* him. I was with his wheel. His personal business is not my concern."

She thought of something else. "Did he seem curious about the village?" *Or me?*

"As I said, we did not idly chat. I had work to do, woman."

Sadly, whether she liked it or not, that was the end of it.

The end of Mr. Waters.

Chapter Seven

"You're daydreaming again," Sadie said.

Esther tore her gaze from the shop window. "Hmm?"

"You've spent more time looking outside the past two days than you've spent the entire time I've known you. Are you waiting for something?"

Someone. Esther pulled her eyes away from the square and her mind away from the daydream. Reluctantly.

"I'm sorry to be distracted." Then she lied. "I don't know why."

Sadie wiped crumbs off the counter. "I thought you'd be brimming over with plans for your wedding."

Me, too.

"By the by, what is the date of it?"

"We haven't decided."

"I imagine Chester wants to be married sooner rather than later."

He did. Chester repeatedly brought up the subject. Esther hedged, giving lame excuses about wishing to enjoy the time of their betrothal, wanting to create the perfect day for such a momentous event.

The truth was, she needed time to wait. For something.

Someone.

"Let me know if I can help," Sadie said. She tied a cloth around a pie and did the same for another, tying each with a knot. "Here you are. Tell Lady Tomkins hello."

"I will." Today, more than any other Thursday, Esther was eager to talk to Verd. Isolated as she was, had Verd heard about Esther and Chester's betrothal? Esther hoped against it, because it wasn't Chester she wished to discuss. Maybe Verd knew of a Mr. Waters.

A half hour later, Esther was welcomed into Verd's parlor with the usual hospitality. Christopher was scratched behind the ears, and Esther was invited to sit in a nearby chair. She set her bonnet on her lap.

But then she noticed there was a second chair pulled close. "You have another guest coming?" She was disappointed at the thought. Her topic of the day was too personal for sharing beyond her friend's ears.

"I do indeed," Verd said with a grin. "Henry?"

Esther recognized the name as the nephew's, but when she turned toward the doorway, she was stunned to see that the man who entered was none other than—

"Mr. Waters?"

His eyebrows raised. "Mrs. Horton?"

"You two know each other?" Verd asked.

"We met by accident," she explained.

"Quite literally," he said. "Remember I told you about the wheel of my carriage?"

Verd looked between the two of them. "Why didn't you say you'd met my Esther?"

He sat in the appointed chair. "Because I didn't know she was your Esther. She was introduced by Mr. Mayfield as Mrs. Horton. And if you remember, Auntie, you kept me busy all of yesterday with bookwork and business."

"Indeed I did," she conceded. "But now you can meet properly. And a good time for it too, for I have been singing your praises, one to the other."

"She thinks very highly of you," Esther said, enjoying his close proximity.

"And you," he said.

A silent moment passed between them. She felt heady looking upon his face, the face of the man in her daydreams, the man who refused to leave her thoughts.

Her bonnet slipped from her lap to the floor, and the two of them bent to retrieve it, their fingers once again touching, making Esther want more.

"Well, well," Verd said.

Esther returned the bonnet to her lap and felt herself blush. It was disconcerting to know their connection was so easily noticed.

Suddenly Verd stood—she never stood during their meetings—and Henry stood in deference. "Sit, sit," she told him. "I will check on the tea."

As she left the room, the couple shared another moment of silence—this one awkward.

"Subtlety is not your aunt's strongest suit," Esther said.

"It is not. But. . .do you mind?"

"Not at all. It is good to have a chance to speak with you beyond the wheel problem, beyond its resolution."

"I agree." He moved to the mantel, fingered a porcelain bird in passing, then faced her.

Esther appreciated seeing the whole of him. As she'd noticed before, he was tall and lean, two attributes that showed his waistcoat and breeches to their full favor. He stood with the confidence of one who was used to addressing others, and his countenance offered her his full attention, as if her presence and her words were the most important details of his day. She willingly gave in kind, quite willing to be lured into his realm—a realm that felt regal yet relaxed.

He cleared his throat. "When we first parted, when I proceeded to town and you in the other direction, I chided myself in the strongest fashion that I had not asked your name."

"I suffered the same chiding," she said.

He let the bird be. "So what if we begin again? I have met you and you have met me, and so. . ."

And so we are free to explore. . . "Verd says you recently obtained a headmaster position in Manchester."

"I did." He returned to his chair and angled it toward hers.

The scent of manly spice made her feel warm inside.

"The Hillston Preparatory School for Boys."

"No girls?"

"Alas, no."

"But you are not against the education of females?"

"I am not. I encourage it. If only society would catch up to modern thinking on the matter."

"I commend your modern thinking—for it matches mine. There should be more purpose in a woman's life than reading approved books, having children, running a household, and supporting a husband's endeavors at the expense of her own."

He smiled. "Such as running a pie shop?"

"Exactly like running a pie shop."

"My aunt said you are a widow. I am sorry for your loss."

"Thank you. Stephen was a very good man."

"But she didn't say. . . Do you have children?"

"I have a stepdaughter, Petunia. Her mother died soon after her birth, and she was eight when I married Stephen. She herself was recently married and has moved to London."

"The next step will be grandchildren, then."

She waved her hands. "I pray not too soon. Although I enjoy the idea of being a grandmother, I am only one and forty." She put a hand over her mouth. "Oh dear. A woman is not supposed to reveal her age—especially at first meeting."

"Third meeting actually."

"Indeed it is. So perhaps it is acceptable." She grinned. "As I have revealed, so must you."

"I am not quite forty."

She laughed. "A younger man."

"Only barely."

Then she realized her *faux pas*. "Forgive me, for my comment about your age compared to mine assumes. . ."

His voice softens. "I must admit I like the assumption."

A wave of pleasure embraced her.

Verd came in the room with Nelly carrying the tea tray. She took her seat, and Christopher immediately appeared and took his. "So then. Have you become fast friends as yet?"

He answered for them. "I believe we have."

She handed Esther a cup, and then served Henry.

Although Esther wanted to know more about him, she was hesitant to ask personal questions with the eager Verd as a witness, so she chose a broader subject. "Although I have been friends with Verd for years, I would love to hear more about your family as a whole. Where did you grow up? Do you have siblings? Are your parents still living?"

"Right to the point," Verd said.

Esther felt her face redden. Although the questions were innocent, they were notably personal. "Forgive me. I have never met any of Verd's relatives beyond her son—and that was years ago."

"She wants to know our family secrets," Verd said.

"I want to know no such thing." But Esther smiled. "Unless they are titillating and riveting."

Henry chuckled then leaned close in confidence. "I have an aversion to rabbits."

"Rabbits?"

"He does," Verd said. "Completely and utterly."

"To eating them, or in general?"

"I believe the one caused the other."

"He got sick once after eating rabbit."

"I have avoided them ever since."

Esther studied their faces. When she saw hints of their smiles, she knew she'd been had. "You are teasing me."

"Absolutely," he said.

"It's quite enjoyable," Verd said.

"Is this a delaying tactic for answering my too-many questions about your family?" she asked.

"Just a diversion." Henry sipped his tea then set the cup on the small table between them. "Perhaps we diverted the conversation because our family is rather ordinary. No recent scandals. And on the reverse, no accomplishments to impress the world."

"Ordinary can possess elements of extraordinary," Esther said.

He shrugged. "To get to the root of it, my parents are living."

"His mother is my sister."

"I have three siblings—two sisters and a brother. They all live in London."

"So you are the lone sheep, lost to Manchester?" It did seem odd he would leave the rest of them.

"If I may be blunt?"

"Please." She braced herself.

"All of my siblings are happily married, and I have six nieces and nephews."

"How nice. I am an only child and my parents have died, so I will never have such a blessing."

His face turned serious. "The happy marriages and children are enormous blessings, blessings that have eluded me to the point of envy." His face reddened, and he avoided her gaze. "I could never confess such a thing to them."

"Only to me," Verd said. "I hear his confessions and he, mine."

"I thought you confessed to me," Esther teased.

"I have so many sins, I need two sets of willing ears." She stroked Christopher's back, then said, "It must be stated that Henry's unmarried status is not due to lack of female interest."

"I would never think such a thing," Esther said with complete sincerity.

"It is simply due to his discerning nature," Verd said.

"I am choosy."

"Pickity-snickity," Verd said.

"I do not believe in marriage for its own sake. I believe God does the choosing."

What a refreshing opinion. "So. . ." Esther said. "If two people get married, it is God's doing?"

"Not at all," Verd said. "People can make mistakes."

Henry nodded once. "God will let two people find each other, and He ignites a spark between them. It is their choice whether they fan the flame or extinguish it."

She liked his reasoning. "So you have not yet felt a spark?"

He retrieved his tea cup and sipped around his answer. "Perhaps."

"Perhaps indeed," Verd said.

Esther was pleased with their answer. If he had said "Not until now," she would have been overwhelmed — even if she had an inkling it *was* his full reply.

A question surfaced. "Do you believe God has chosen *one* spouse for each person?" *What about me? God brought Stephen and me together. If I marry Chester. . .if I marry. . .*

"I believe," Henry said quietly, "there are seasons to life. A marriage made in youth may only be for that season. But I believe it is possible that God can and will choose another spouse for the one left behind, so the two can travel through the next season together."

Out of nowhere, Esther felt tears threaten and hurriedly set her tea aside and ran from the parlor into the dining room.

She overheard Henry say, "I'm so sorry. Did I say something wrong?"

"Not at all," Verd said. "I'll go after her."

Before Verd appeared, Esther swiped her tears away. "I'm so sorry," she told her friend.

"As a widow, you *can* find happiness again."

"I know. And I appreciate his words."

"As do I. For they sound like truth." Verd handed her a handkerchief.

"I've made a fool of myself."

"I assure you, you have not. If anything, you have piqued Henry's interest — more than it is already piqued."

"But I shouldn't do that!"

Verd looked at her askance. "And why not?"

Because I am betrothed to Chester!

Esther kept that truth to herself and said instead, "I have only met Henry, and here we are talking of husbands and wives and God doing the choosing. . ."

"When last here, you mentioned Chester's persistent interest. Do you think God chose him for you?"

It was the question of the century. "I don't know."

Verd took the handkerchief and dabbed Esther's cheek. "Then it behooves you to wait until you *do* know. Until then, let us finish our tea."

Esther took a deep breath, calming her unease. "I *would* like to make amends for my outburst."

"T'will not be difficult. Let us go discuss the details of my upcoming party."

**

Esther left Verd's home with an invitation to come pick the berries from Verd's garden tomorrow evening—with Henry to help her.

Although she knew she should have declined the offer, she could not. And did not.

Her walk back to the shop was made without conscious thought. One foot found its way in front of the other, her breath moved in and out, and her destination was reached without the realization that time had passed.

"Did Verd like her pies?" Sadie asked upon Esther's entrance.

"As usual."

"Any interesting news?"

"It was an ordinary visit." Esther felt guilty for the immensity of the lie. But she did not correct it.

Chapter Eight

Chester came in at closing time, on his way to the Boar's Head for his Friday night ritual of ale and friends. Esther had never minded before and certainly did not mind on this particular Friday.

He kissed her on the cheek. "I will see you tomorrow."

She was glad he did not ask her how she was going to spend her evening. She didn't wish to lie to him—even though she *was* lying by her omission.

After closing the shop, Esther rushed home to put on another dress, the one patterned with pink rosebuds. She combed through her hair and refastened it into a bun at the nape of her neck. She pinched her cheeks but found them already blushed with anticipation. Then she carefully set her bonnet and tied the pink ribbon in a pretty bow to the side. She peered at herself in the mirror above her bureau. "What are you doing, Esther Horton?"

She looked away, unable to look herself in the eye.

**

"Do you often pick berries here?" Mr. Waters asked as they took their baskets into Verd's garden.

"Never before this evening. Your aunt usually has Sam bring me the bounty."

"But today she is making you do the work."

"I don't mind at all." She heard the deeper meaning in her words, and added. "I have grown to love gardening."

"You did not always love it?"

"Not at all. My late husband was the one who had a passion for it. He was never happier than in his garden, planting, weeding, watering, or picking the harvest."

"A man of the earth."

"Completely. Though he grew up in Manchester, his heart belonged to the countryside."

"And to you."

"And to me."

They began at a row of blackberry bushes, each taking a side. "So you grew to enjoy it?"

"I have. Actually, I think the Almighty had a plan."

"He is known to use gardens." He winked.

She ate a berry. "Our payment for the work."

"A fine pay it is." He ate his own berry. "So what plan did God implement in your garden?"

"I hesitate to say, because it may seem presumptuous to suppose upon God's deeds."

"There is no way for us to fully know the extent of His ways in this world. But I do not believe He objects to us seeing His hand."

She stooped to get the berries at the bottom of the bush, which gave her slight cover for her story. "I would never have gardened if not for Stephen. And after he died, it turns out I needed the garden for my very survival."

"The pie shop."

She nodded. "We had some money saved from his time as the estate manager for your aunt, but I realized that money would run out. I did not wish to rely on the charity of others, so I needed to do *something*. One evening while Petunia and I were eating a pie I'd made, she remarked on its tastiness and told me I should make them to sell." Esther stood and faced him straight across the bush. "And so I did. The shop has saved me from poverty and provided me diversion and satisfaction."

"I believe it has also provided the whole of Chancebury with the latter."

"At the risk of boasting, I believe you are right."

In concert, they moved to the next bush. Then Mr. Waters said, "I believe God sent me to Manchester."

"What were your clues?"

"A door closed."

"In what way?"

"The school where I was teaching in London hired a new headmaster. It is fair to say we did not agree on our methods."

"I ask again, in what way?"

"He believed boys could be forced to learn by using a ruler in ways other than its original purpose."

"He hit them?"

"With gusto. And pleasure, I believe."

"How despicable."

"I attempted to get him to change his ways but was dismissed for my efforts." He spread a hand. "A door closed."

"And one opened in Manchester?"

"It did."

"Why Manchester? There are many miles between it and London."

"Nearly two hundred, I believe." He popped another berry in his mouth and seemed to ponder his next words. "Two hundred miles was not too far for God. The opportunity presented itself over mutton chops and Banbury cakes. I was dining at my sister's one evening while they were entertaining a friend, a Mr. Connelly."

"Who happened to live in Manchester?"

He smiled. "You jump ahead."

"Forgive me. Continue."

"His son attended Hillston in Manchester, and he noted that the headmaster was retiring due to ill health. The subject of my situation was mentioned, and by the last bite of cake, it was arranged for me to travel back to Manchester with him, to interview for the position."

Esther hung her basket on her arm and applauded. "Bravo, Mr. Connelly."

"Bravo, God."

She retrieved a fallen berry and dropped it in her basket. "I like how you see God's hand."

"How we both see God's hand."

"I fear I have been lax in that regard these past years."

"You have been busy raising a child. Surviving."

She shook her head. "That is a poor excuse." Esther swiped a hair away from her eyes with the back of her hand. "Stephen was the godly one. He taught me by example more than words."

"I wish I could have met him."

She studied him a moment. "He would have liked you."

"And I, him?"

Esther nodded with complete certainty. "You have much in common."

"How so?"

She suddenly feared she'd said too much, for in actuality her knowledge of Mr. Waters was limited. "You are both honorable men who stand up for what you believe in. You both seek God and love Him."

He put a finger to the brim of his hat. "Thank you, Mrs. Horton. I appreciate the generous words."

"You're welcome."

"But I believe there is more we have in common."

"And what's that?"

"We both enjoy the company of. . ."

Oh dear. He's going to say it!

He winked, and tossed a berry in his mouth. "We enjoy the company of delicious fruit."

"Oh, you." She couldn't help but feel a tad bit disappointed.

**

Mr. Waters stood on the bench of the wagon, took Esther's hand, and helped her up to the seat beside him. The bed of the wagon was loaded with baskets and crates full of berries, apples, carrots, cabbages, and green beans.

"I can't believe we picked such a bounty," Esther said.

"I can't believe it is near dark," Mr. Waters said. "The time flew by."

"Good conversation and hard work will do that."

He took up the reins, but then Verd came outside. "Wait!"

Esther was shocked twofold: at the sight of her friend outside her home *and* hearing her shout.

"What's wrong, Auntie?"

She took a moment to catch her breath, her hand to her chest. Then she said, "I wish to order a blackberry pie from Esther."

That was the reason for her sudden appearance and shout? "Very well," Esther said. "Next Thursday, I will make a blackberry —"

"Not next Thursday," Verd said. "Tomorrow. For it is Henry's favorite pie."

"That it is," Henry said.

"Then I will make you one," she told him with a nod.

But Verd wasn't through. "Bring it over when you come for dinner."

Previously, sharing tea had been the extent of Verd's hospitality. "Dinner?"

"You do eat dinner, don't you?" Verd asked.

"Of course I do, but—"

"Then join us for dinner tomorrow evening." Verd turned toward the front door, but kept talking. "And bring the pie." The door closed behind her.

"It appears I am coming to dinner," she said.

Mr. Waters chucked at the horses. "I, for one, look forward to it."

**

Dark had tucked the world in shadows as Esther and Mr. Waters unloaded the garden's abundance.

She lit a candle in the pie shop— which was closed for the day.

"Sadie will be so surprised when she comes in tomorrow morning," she said, placing the last basket of blackberries on a table.

He turned in a circle. "So this is where the deliciousness happens."

"It is," Esther said.

"Where is the oven?"

"Come, I'll show you." She took up the candle and led him into the back room that had been built to allow access to the front of the oven, while the bulk of said oven remained outdoors. "Sadie comes in very early to get the fire hot enough for the baking."

"How does she know what hot is hot enough?"

Esther shrugged. "Experience. I am lucky to —"

"Esther?"

She turned to see Myrtle Cray in the doorway. Her stomach flipped. "Good evening, Myrtle."

"I saw the wagon outside, and then a flickering within." She gazed at Mr. Waters, top to bottom. "Are you the man with the broken wheel?"

"I am he. Mr. Waters." He offered her a small bow. "And you are?"

She bobbed an awkward curtsy. "Miss Cray."

"A pleasure."

But it wasn't a pleasure. Who knew how Myrtle would skew this moment?

"If you'll excuse me?" he said with a tip of his hat. He bowed to Esther, too, and she was ever so glad he didn't say, "See you tomorrow."

As they heard the wagon pull away, Myrtle asked, "Where is he staying?"

Although Esther was tempted to lie, she told the truth—or a portion of it. "At Coventry Hall, I believe."

"Where is he from?"

Enough truth. "If you see him again, you will have to ask. Now, if you will excuse me, I need to get home." She blew out the light and held the door for Myrtle. "Good night, then."

"But—"

Esther hurried away before more questions could be asked.

Chapter Nine

Esther went to the pie shop early, knowing the work of handling the cornucopia of produce from Verd's garden. She was hulling her second bowl of raspberries, remembering the pleasure of the picking, when Sadie came in.

Sadie's eyes grew wide. "Where did all this come from?"

"Lady Tomkins's garden."

She ate a berry. "She must have had every available lad in the county picking."

"Just me," Esther said, "And her visiting nephew."

"It must have taken hours and hours."

"Until nearly dark." She needed the conversation to move on. "Since much bounty demands much work, I came in early."

Sadie put on her apron. "Let's get to it, then."

"Also, to let you know, Lady Tomkins ordered a blackberry pie for today."

"It isn't Thursday."

"Apparently her nephew likes pie."

Sadie tucked her hair beneath a cap. "Good for him. Good for us."

"I. . ." Should she say it? "I have been invited to dine with them this evening."

"At the hall?"

"Yes."

"You've never dined there before, have you?"

"No."

"How odd."

If only Esther hadn't said anything.

**

Esther looked up from her work when Chester came in. "Your pie is ready."

He took offense. "No 'good day'? No kiss on the cheek?"

She chastised herself for treating him like any other customer. She had to pull her head out of the clouds and act normally. She took his pie off the shelf and handed it to him—adding a kiss to his cheek.

He held the pie to his nose. "What kind today?"

"Mutton with cabbage, carrots, and onions."

"Sounds tasty."

Sadie stepped in from the oven room. "Afternoon, Chester."

"Sadie."

She looked to Esther. "Lady Tomkins's blackberry pie is just out."

"A pie for the hall? It's not Thursday," Chester said.

It seemed everyone knew the schedule. "Her nephew is visiting."

"Esther is going there for dinner," Sadie said.

Esther felt herself blush. Why had she told Sadie about the invitation?

"Dinner?" Chester asked.

She busied herself rolling out a crust. "I was as surprised as you. I have never been invited for a meal." She hoped her words minimized the event. "I believe I am invited for my contribution to the dinner conversation."

"So her nephew is dull?"

Not at all. "I believe he is a teacher."

"Dull."

"That is unduly harsh."

"I dislike people who know books but don't know real life."

"One does not have to negate the other."

He shrugged.

She knew she should let it go, but had one more question. "I am curious. Who in Chancebury knows books but not real life?"

He was saved from an answer when Myrtle swept into the shop like a foul wind. "Afternoon, Esther. Chester. Sadie."

The woman avoided Esther's gaze, which usually meant she had gossip on her mind — about Esther.

"What can I do for you today, Myrtle?"

Her eyes scanned the pies cooling on a shelf. "You work far too hard, Esther. Being here even after dark last night. . ."

Esther's stomach flipped. "I do what must be done."

Chester took the bait. "You were here after dark?"

Myrtle beat Esther to the answer. "It was well past dark when I spotted a lone candle flickering in the shop. I thought it odd, so investigated and found Esther and Mr. Waters here. Together." Her jowls twitched.

"Waters?" Chester asked. "The man with the wheel?"

"The same," Esther said. "He helped me unload produce from Lady Tomkins's garden."

"How does he know Lady Tomkins?"

"Yes, Esther," Myrtle said. "You never did specify."

There was no circumventing the truth. "Mr. Waters is Lady Tomkins's nephew. Just visiting."

Myrtle twirled the ribbon of her bonnet around a finger and grinned. The action of an ingénue looked ridiculous considering her fifty-some years. "He is quite handsome. Is he married?"

"I don't believe so."

Luckily, Chester had little patience for small talk. "I best be getting back to the forge." He tipped his hat and left with his pie.

Esther let a breath of relief escape before asking, "Which pie would you like, Myrtle?"

The woman spun around toward the door. "None today. Ta-ta."

Esther let the air settle. "That, I didn't need."

"That?" Sadie asked.

"Nothing." Only it wasn't nothing. At all.

**

Why do I blush every time I see him?

"It looks delicious." Mr. Waters eyed the blackberry pie Esther carried into Coventry Hall. "Can we eat dessert first tonight?"

"You most certainly cannot," Nelly said, taking possession of it. "I spent all day cooking a nice meal for you, and you will do nothing to curb your appetite before it is served."

He saluted her. "Yes, ma'am."

She turned on her heel and left them.

"I think she likes you," Esther said.

"How can you tell?"

"If she scolds you, she thinks of you as family."

"I *am* family."

"There you are."

"My aunt is waiting in the parlor," he said.

"Impatiently waiting," came Verd's voice from the next room.

Esther entered and kissed her friend on the cheek. "Patience is a virtue," she said.

"I have never claimed to be virtuous," Verd said. "Sit now, you two. Let us have a nice chat before Nelly calls us to dine."

Esther noticed an open book on the small table beside Verd's settee. "What are you reading?"

She put a hand upon it. "*A Vindication of the Rights of Woman.* Henry lent it to me."

Esther had not heard of it. "Rights of women? Are you a radical thinker, Mr. Waters?"

He pointed to his head. "I am a rational thinker who believes women are, too."

"Now that *is* radical," Esther said.

Verd adjusted Christopher's paws upon her lap. "Henry says women have the same ability to reason as men do."

"Mrs. Wollstonecraft says that, in her book," he explained.

"Of course we do. It's only logical," Esther said.

"You prove the point," he said. "But she goes further in saying that because of that fact, women deserve the same rights as men."

"Namely?"

"The right to an education for one."

Esther tossed her hands in the air. "I have been touting that for years. Females are not born to be mindless, emotional creatures, yet we are encouraged to be just that. We have good minds, and God wants us to use them."

Verd applauded. "Well said, Esther. I wish I had been allowed to voice my opinions. I would have liked to be a true partner to my husband."

"He would not allow it?" Mr. Waters asked.

"He believed I existed for his pleasure."

"And not your own," Esther said, remembering Verd's stories of oppression.

"Not my own. At all." Verd's face had turned haggard.

"It makes me so sad for you," Esther said.

"I survived it."

"But you shouldn't have merely survived, but thrived. Women are more than pretty faces and polite manners."

"Indeed you are, and I am glad for it," Mr. Waters said.

She was taken aback. "Why?"

"Because women who reveal an innate intelligence—like you and my aunt—inspire me to be a better man. We should be *more* together than apart."

Verd snuggled Christopher under her chin, making him purr. "My husband encouraged me to be weak, frivolous, and silent on all subjects outside the doors of this house. If I questioned him on any issue beyond the domestic, he suggested I calm myself and retire to my room lest I become agitated."

Esther shook her head. "He wished for you to remain mute and ignorant."

"Completely. One time I chose a volume from our library on the history of English kings, and he snatched it away from me, forbidding me to read it. To this day I remember his words: 'There is no reason for you to know what came before this moment. Nor should you worry for the future. Focus on today, on my dinner, our son, and the betterment of our household.'"

"Those are also admirable tasks," Mr. Waters said.

"But I could do more, think more, be more." Verd's voice rose, causing Christopher to escape her lap.

Mr. Waters pointed toward the book. "That is why you will appreciate Mrs. Wollstonecraft's book."

"I already do."

"I would like to read it, too," Esther said. "Stephen often brought home books from the hall, and we'd read them together."

"Did you read them to your daughter?" he asked.

"We tried to teach Petunia—in all subjects, in all ways. But she was not interested. Perhaps if there had been a real school in Chancebury, she might have been willing to learn." Or not.

"I will see you get the book when

Auntie is through with it." He smoothed his trouser against his leg. "Tell me more about your husband, Mrs. Horton."

She thought a moment, trying to think of how to best describe Stephen. "He was kind, capable—"

Verd interrupted her list. "He was a first-rate estate manager. And he was invaluable after Thomas was killed and we had the difficulties with the debt he had incurred."

"Stephen enjoyed working at the hall, though more for its sake than your husband's, I'm afraid."

"No one liked Thomas. It is a fact I cannot and will not dispute. But back to Stephen's attributes."

The mental list was long, but Esther chose a highlight. "Beyond his abilities and character, he adored me. And I him."

Verd put her hands to her chest. "Oh, my. To be adored. . .there can be nothing more fulfilling."

Esther looked to her lap, thinking of Stephen's smile, his soft touch, his encouraging words. "He never made me feel like 'just a woman,' but instead as if we were joined together, two for one, moving through life." She glanced up and saw Mr. Waters nodding.

"Everything you have told me about him confirms him to be an exceptional man."

"That he was."

Nelly entered, wiping her hands on her apron. "Dinner is served."

Mr. Waters helped his aunt to her feet, and she wrapped a hand around one of his arms. He offered his other arm to Esther and led them toward the dining room.

"I am the luckiest of all men this night," he said, "to be in the company of two beautiful, intelligent women."

Esther felt rather lucky herself.

**

After dinner, Mr. Waters drove Esther home.

"Is something wrong?" he asked. "You have grown quiet."

Everything is wrong. Even while everything is right.

"I must be tired," she said. "I had a marvelous time this evening."

"As did I. I enjoy a lively discussion."

"As do I." She decided to share one factor of her silence. "Such discussion is a phenomenon I now experience too seldom. My friends do not read much, except the Bible. Perhaps."

"There are many thought-provoking stories in the Bible."

"Which would do well to be discussed."

"Perhaps you could bring them up in conversation?"

She unsuccessfully stifled a laugh and clapped a hand over her mouth. "I apologize. I must seem prideful, raising myself above others. I do have many dear friends." *And one is my fiancé.*

"It is understandable they are focused on the issues of the here and now rather than past history or biblical stories that often take a bit of effort to discover their moral lesson."

He had pegged the main issue. "How do we inspire people to expand their knowledge?"

"By sharing it with them."

"What if they won't listen? What if they change the subject?"

He pulled the reins, stopping the carriage so he could face her. "'Who hath ears to hear, let him hear.'"

Esther remembered numerous times when Chester had cut her off and shut down a conversation that delved into deeper subjects. "What good does it do if they don't hear? Don't listen?"

"We have to keep telling the stories—as Jesus did. Hopefully by repetition, their hearts and eyes will be opened, and they will see the full meaning."

"It's not just Bible stories they avoid, but subjects that are important to our lives right now—and to Chancebury's future. I think of all the children here who know next to nothing, not even how to read. We need a school for them. A simple school. Nothing fancy. But somewhere where they can learn something beyond how to feed a chicken or dip a candle."

"Those are also important tasks."

She looked to the stars overhead then pointed at them. "I have only to look up to see the expanse of what is available to learn. There is always more."

"Then teach them. Expand the borders of their world."

She chuckled and let her hand fall to her lap. "How can I teach what I myself do not know?"

"Learn it. Then share it."

She loved the idea, but the implementation would be difficult.

"You told me you are teaching Sadie to read, yes?"

"I am."

"Then you can teach others who wish to learn."

"But there is more to life than reading and basic arithmetic."

He raised a finger. "But reading opens the world. Start there. The rest will come."

Esther felt a stirring inside, as though a breeze had blown through an opened door. There were too many logistics to determine, but the idea of learning—and teaching—left her giddy with possibilities.

Once they reached her home, Mr. Waters got down from the carriage and helped her alight. He bowed, and she curtsied, but then she did something more. She extended her hand to him. "Thank you, Mr. Waters. For the fine conversation and for proposing an even finer challenge."

He shook her hand then put his free hand on top, keeping hers captive. "Don't you think it's time to call each other by our given names?"

"I would like that. Thank you, Henry."

"A good night to you, Esther."

She stood by the front door of her cottage until the sound of his carriage faded into nothingness. In the silence, she realized that more than anything in the world—even more than wanting a school or knowledge—she wanted Henry Waters to remain a part of her life.

Chapter Ten

Esther and Chester took a walk after church. She held his arm, but looked ahead, seeing nothing. If someone had covered her eyes and suddenly asked, "Where are you right this moment?" she would not have been able to tell them.

Chester stopped their progress. "Where *are* you today?"

"I'm sorry. My mind is wandering."

"Tell it to come back. I feel as though you don't even need me to be here."

Esther blinked, forcing herself into the present. She touched his cheek. "Again, I apologize."

"Pastor Wilkins's sermon wasn't that thought provoking."

"Actually, I wouldn't know."

"At least I'm not the only one you're ignoring."

She tried to corral her thoughts, but they fled from her like sheep out of a pen.

"How was dinner last night at the hall?"

She ignored the entire subject of Henry and turned to the subject she *could* share with him. "I would like to start a school in Chancebury, for boys *and* girls."

His head drew back. "A school? Whyever for?"

"To educate the children. Too many don't even know how to read. Look at Sadie. She didn't know until I took it upon myself to teach her."

"Does she need to know how to read? Does she have some secret stash of books she's been wanting to read all her life? Does she even own a book?"

"Don't be rude."

"'Tis a logical question. I don't know how to read either, and I've never missed it."

She felt her mouth gape open. "You don't know how to read?"

"I shoe horses and fix wagons. Why would I need to read?"

"To find out more about worlds beyond Chancebury."

"I've been to Manchester. That's enough of the world for me. Too much."

How could he be so utterly closed-minded? Chester disparaged new worlds; Henry embraced them.

Esther embraced them.

Chester kicked a pebble away from the space where he stood, just like he kicked away Esther's idea. "People don't want their children to take time away from chores to learn something they'll never use."

It was her turn to be incredulous. "Even if it means they can better themselves? Or at least tap into the knowledge the world has to share?"

He started walking again. "I'd say 'no thank you' to that."

None too gently, she pulled him to a stop. "Then you are an ignorant fool."

His brow furrowed. "What's got into you, Esther?"

She tried to put a word to it. "Opportunity."

"To stir a pot that doesn't need stirring?"

"I believe it needs a good whipping."

"What about your pies? Are you giving that up—and the income it earns—to create this school no one needs or wants? A school where you'd get paid nothing?"

She'd thought about this. "I don't think it would come to that. I could set up the school in my spare time."

"Where? Where would it be?"

She hesitated. "I don't know."

"Who's going to teach there?"

That was the largest issue. "I could — if I let Sadie take over the shop. Or. . ." She thought of Henry. "Perhaps someone else."

He scoffed. "We know every soul in Chancebury. There isn't a scholar among us."

She knew he was right — which was part of her conundrum. "Perhaps there is a hidden scholar here."

This elicited a full laugh. "I suppose old Mr. Grundsby recites poems while he shears his sheep? And I'm certain the butcher's wife knows all the kings of England in proper order."

"They could."

"No one needs that kind of nonsense in their head. Be practical, Esther.

People in Chancebury need their brains to survive. Nothing more."

He'd quieted the wind in her sail to the point of feeling adrift. "Walk me home, please."

"Nay now, I didn't mean to upset you. I just spoke the truth; you know I did."

He'd spoken *a* truth. That didn't mean there wasn't more truth to be had.

**

Esther closed the book she'd attempted to read all afternoon. Checking the pages, she realized she'd only read two. In an hour. And remembered none of it.

"This is absurd," she told the room.

She bowed her head, needing the peace that only God could provide. "Lord, help me wind my way through my thoughts about the school. It seems like such a good idea. It would be a blessing to many and might give some of the young people hope for a more productive life away from Chancebury."

"They would be able to read My book."

Esther grabbed at the new thought. "They would! They would be able to read the Bible for themselves! Is that not a glorious goal?"

Her thoughts suddenly turned to Chester. He was against the entire notion — which had made her think less of him.

Which in turn made her think more of Henry.

Chester and Henry. Neither man knew of the other beyond passing. Two men who had gained her attention for far different reasons. Chester, because he was someone she'd known forever and was a comfortable, familiar friend who helped her enjoy what was. And Henry, because he was a fascinating man who challenged her mind and made her think of what could be. One was her fiancé, and one was. . .not.

There was the core of it. The full fact of it. To think of Henry and all the things he made her envision — many of which were beyond common reason — was that wise? Or was she being foolish to a fault?

She put her elbows on her knees, grasping her hands in prayer, bowing her head. "Help me see what You want me to see. Help me do what You want me to do. Keep me from mistaking what is exciting and new for Your will. If these thoughts of a school and—and Henry—are not pleasing to You, take them from—"

A knock on the door interrupted her prayer.

When she answered it her heart fluttered. "Mr. Waters. Henry. How nice to see you."

"I hope I do not disturb."

"Not at all."

He held a book. "My aunt has finished Mrs. Wollstonecraft. You mentioned wanting to read it?"

"Why thank you. How thoughtful."

While he stood there, she made a decision. Although she wanted to invite him in, to do so was improper. But that didn't mean she wanted him to leave. "Would you like to sit in the garden with me? It's a beautiful evening."

"I would enjoy that very much. For I leave tomorrow."

"No!" She realized she had overreacted. "Forgive me, but this comes as a surprise." She led him to a bench near a trellis of clematis and sat beside him. Their bodies touched side to side, and she was glad for the contact that could not be avoided by the usual protocol or propriety.

"Leaving was a surprise to me, also," he said.

"What about your aunt's party Wednesday?"

He sighed deeply. "I received word that I was needed at the school for some issue. As I am new at the position, I feel the need to obey their request."

"Of course." The thought of him leaving — even though she'd known his time in Chancebury was temporary — pained her as surely as a slap.

He raised his eyes to gaze at the sky, and then the garden. He closed them and took a deep breath. "There is peace here."

"This is the place I run to when I am unsettled."

"Hmm. Close your eyes and listen."

Although she knew there was the chance of feeling silly, Henry's request seemed anything but. So she closed her eyes. And listened.

"What do you hear?" he asked.

"I hear bees, the wind in the trees, the soft bleating of my neighbor's sheep down the road."

"I hear music."

She opened her eyes. "Music?"

"Are you a fan of Beethoven?"

"Who?"

"He is a composer whose fame is continuing to grow. I happened to hear his *Eroica* Symphony in Vienna two years ago."

"Vienna," she said wistfully. "I cannot imagine such a place."

"You have not traveled?"

She touched her temple. "Only in here. Though I long to. Stephen and I often talked about going to the Continent once Petunia was grown." She sighed. "But then he died, and the dream was set aside."

"It need not be. Perhaps postponed?"

She knew the next would sound presumptuous. "I have no one to travel with, no one to help with the logistics of it, nor anyone who has the desire for it."

"Perhaps your daughter — ?"

She laughed. "Petunia is busy with her new life as a married woman — as she should be. The last thing she would want is to travel with her mother."

He gave her a simple nod then raised his face and closed his eyes again. "When I hear glorious music I like to close my eyes and let the music surround me. I give it free rein to create images in my head that are far beyond the here and now."

"I have never heard a symphony or any music besides hymns and local folk songs."

He studied her. "I would love to share music with you. And more, for there is so much in the world to experience. And it is better experienced with. . .with someone."

Esther longed to spring to her feet and say, *"Yes! Let me go with you! Let me be that someone!"*

Instead, the knowledge that there was no chance for any of it to become reality, caused her imagined spring to turn into the simple act of standing.

"Shall we walk?" she asked, knowing of nothing else she could say.

"Of course."

She led him through her rows of flowers. Her heart pounded in her chest, revealing what her body understood and her mind would never acknowledge.

She loved Henry Waters. She wanted Henry Waters to love her. She wanted to marry Henry Waters.

She leaned over to pinch a dead blossom, letting the words that needed to be said find their voice. "I need to tell you something, Henry. Something I should have told you a long time ago."

"What is that?"

When she straightened to face him, her balance bobbled, and she would have fallen if Henry had not reached out to steady her.

"Thank you. I'm so clumsy." But as she righted herself, she spotted Myrtle standing at the corner of her fence. "Evening, Myrtle."

The smile that crossed the woman's face spoke volumes as to the mischievous workings of her thoughts. "Evening, Esther. And Mr. Waters, is it?"

Henry tipped his hat. "Good evening, ma'am."

"Miss," she said.

"I stand corrected. Good evening, miss."

"Mr. Waters stopped by to lend me a book," Esther said, realizing too late her explanation would only add to Myrtle's smoldering fire.

"I see."

"I should be leaving," Henry said.

"No need to hurry off on my account," Myrtle said.

"I'm not. It is getting late, and I must get back to the hall." He nodded toward Myrtle. "Good evening, miss." Then turned to Esther. "Mrs. Horton."

And he was away.

All that was within her wished to run after him. *Don't go, Henry! You're leaving tomorrow! I need you to stay! I need you to know the truth about me and Chester, and. . .*

I need you to love me anyway.

Myrtle stood at the fence and watched him go. "A bit unusual, me seeing you two together at odd hours, not once, but twice."

Esther felt the full weight of her predicament. If she explained it would seem she protested out of guilt. Yet to say nothing would hint at that same.

The latter seemed the lesser of two evils. "Good evening, Myrtle."

She escaped inside her cottage. Upon the click of the door, her legs gave out beneath her, and she slipped to the floor like a puddle.

"Lord, what shall I do?"

Chapter Eleven

Sleep eluded her.

Esther turned over in bed and opened her eyes to the morning, which had come too soon.

Although she longed to know God's will in her life, and usually had a good sense about it due to the peace that was its companion, last night's sleep — or lack thereof — seemed a good indication that her current situation was not God's will.

She surrendered to that truth. Yet she still wasn't certain what came next.

Did God disapprove of her tenuous situation with Chester? Her own doubts hinted that the Almighty might be against their match.

Or did God disapprove of her burgeoning feelings for Henry?

She found herself smiling. The sudden appearance of Henry in her life did not seem a coincidence. Coming upon him on the road with a broken wheel, perhaps. But being caught in the rain with him inside the carriage, seeing him at Verd's. . .

If she had decided to visit Stephen's grave an hour earlier or later, she would have missed meeting him altogether. If his wheel had not broken just then, if the rain had not forced them to take cover — a rain that ended soon after. . .

She might have met him at Verd's when he came to visit, but would meeting in that formal situation have sparked the same intensity of feelings?

Was there a reason she hadn't married Chester yet, or even set a date?

If she weren't betrothed to Chester, would she rush into Henry's arms?

Would he want her there?

She threw aside the covers and sat on the side of the bed. "You are a fickle woman, Esther Horton. Fickle and vain. Two men cannot — cannot — be in love with you. It is impossible." She looked heavenward. "Forgive me if I've offended You in any way, Father. I mean no harm to either man, so help me. Thy will be done."

**

Esther crimped the edge of a beef pie and slit the crust with steam holes. "Another one, ready," she called out to Sadie.

"Coming."

Esther moved to slit the next two pies, a strawberry and a raspberry. She looked up as Sam came in.

"Sam. Is everything all right at the hall?"

"Right as rain." He handed her a folded note with a seal on it. "Mr. Waters asked me to bring this by for you."

She held it to her breast. "Has he left for Manchester yet?"

"First thing this morning."

He is really gone then. "Thank you, Sam. Let Lady Tomkins know the pies will be ready for her party Wednesday."

He tipped his cap and was gone.

Sadie came out of the oven room, swiping her forehead against its heat. She spotted the note. "Who's that from?"

Esther hedged. "Coventry Hall. If you don't mind?" She nodded toward the door, stepped outside, and sat on the bench beneath the window. Before breaking the seal, she ran a finger over her name. *Esther* was written in a beautiful cursive with extra embellishments on the E. "Henry," she whispered.

"Morning, Esther," said the butcher's wife.

"Morning."

Luckily, the woman moved on, but the square had come alive with people going about their business. Esther best get on with it before someone stopped and asked about the note.

She unfolded it and read:

Dearest Esther,

I hope you forgive me the endearment, but I found I could not write this note without including it. For despite our short acquaintance, you have become very dear to me.

I can honestly say that I have never met another woman — yea, another person — who has given me so much pleasure by their mere presence. That presence would be enough in itself, yet it is enhanced by the blessed contribution of good conversation about subjects near and far, and dialogue that ignites new ideas and deepens old ones.

I regret missing my aunt's party and having to return to Manchester so soon. Too soon.

May God grant us the joy of another meeting in the very near future.

Yours truly,
Henry

A wave of grief engulfed her, and she felt tears threaten. She bowed her head. *Lord, what shall I do? His words mean the world to me.*

"A distressing note, Esther?"

She looked up. Why was she doomed to see Myrtle around every corner?

She quickly slipped the note into her apron pocket. "I am not distressed."

"You looked so. You looked very much so. You had your head bowed and—"

"Perhaps I was taking a nap."

Myrtle shook her head violently. "I watched you reading the note, and then you bowed your head. There was no time for a nap."

Esther stood and glared at her. "Have you nothing better to do than trace my every move?"

Myrtle held her gaze. "Not every move—though who knows what mischief has occurred beyond my gaze."

"What mischief could ever occur beyond your gaze, Myrtle Cray?"

With that, Esther went inside the shop.

Sadie was there to meet her, an incredulous look upon her face. "I cannot believe you said that to her. She deserved that, and more, but..."

In the moment between outside and in, Esther had regained her senses. "Oh dear. What have I done?"

"No good, that is for certain," Sadie said. "You know Myrtle lets no slight go unpunished."

Esther put a protective hand upon her pocket. "I have done nothing wrong." *In public or private, yet I have sinned aplenty in my heart.*

"The truth doesn't matter," Sadie said. "You know that. Myrtle can take a speck of dust and create a blinding dust cloud."

Esther looked out to the square. "Did you see in which direction she went?"

Sadie pointed to the left. Toward Chester's smithy. Then she said, "Go make amends. And be quick about it."

Esther ran out of the shop, and tried—as unobtrusively as possible—to hurry toward Chester's. She received curious looks, but dared not lessen her pace. Her future depended on reaching Chester before Myrtle did.

She turned the final corner and spotted the two of them together. Unfortunately, Myrtle was doing all the talking, gesticulating toward the pie shop.

Chester looked up and spotted Esther. She forced herself to smile and wave as though nothing were amiss.

Unfortunately, when Myrtle saw her, she stormed to her side. "Come now, Esther, it's time you tell Chester — your betrothed — about your secret liaisons with Mr. Waters."

Esther let her brow dip — hoping her expression feigned surprise. "Secret liaisons? I hardly think dining with Lady Tomkins or feeding Mr. Waters' curiosity about the pie oven deserves such a phrase."

"I saw you together at your cottage."

Esther forced herself to remain calm. "Outside my cottage. In my garden, to be exact."

Chester spoke up. "He was at your cottage?"

"In my garden. He was kind enough to bring over a book he and Lady Tomkins wished for me to read."

"What book?"

Oh dear. *A Vindication of the Rights of Woman* was not the title of an easily enjoyed novel. "A book by a Mrs. Wollstonecraft."

"What a name," Chester said.

Esther shrugged. "She is the one who must endure it."

"Sounds made up," Myrtle said.

"You would know about made-up things," Esther said.

She huffed and fuddled. "Well, I. . ."

Chester remained true to his dislike of gossip and took Myrtle by the shoulders, spun her around, and gave her a little push. "On with you, woman. Mind your own house before sullying someone else's."

"But—"

"Go!"

She scurried away, murmuring to herself.

Esther tried to calm herself. "I'm sorry you had to endure her nonsense. You met Mr. Waters. He's a gentleman beyond reproach."

"I met him long enough to fix a wheel."

"Well, let me assure you, he is a man of honor."

"How do you know that?"

She thought quickly. "Lady Tomkins has always spoken highly of him. He just took a headmaster position in Manchester. The term begins soon."

"Good. So he will not be coming back to Chancebury often." He hesitated, then added, "We wouldn't want to fuel Myrtle's imagination."

"Indeed not," Esther said. She kissed his cheek. "I best get back to the baking."

He called after her. "She mentioned a note?"

Esther nearly put a hand on her pocket but stopped the action in time. "I received a note from Mr. Waters, telling me goodbye. He has already left for Manchester."

"May I read it?" He glanced at her apron. "I see the outline of something in your pocket."

"I hardly think that's necessary."

He cleared his throat. "I do. For the note is not Myrtle's doing. It is paper I can feel and words I can read." He held out his hand.

She handed the note to him, her mind racing, trying to remember the words that were said. *Dearest Esther. . .dear to me. . .pleasure. . .good conversation. . .joy. . .see you again. . .*

But then a reprieve.

Chester looked at the letter and handed it back to her. "I forgot. I can't read."

A nervous laugh escaped. "Well, let me assure you that—"

"Read it to me."

Esther felt her breath leave her. There was no choice but to edit the words between eye and mouth. Not of their content but of their intimacy.

"Dear Mrs. Horton." She sped past the entire first paragraph, summing it up thusly, "It was a pleasure to meet you. I enjoyed talking with you about books and travel. Feel free to borrow other books from my aunt. I will try to keep her supplied. I wish I did not have to return to Manchester so soon and miss my aunt's party. I am nervous about my new position. Hopefully, we can meet again. Signed, Mr. Henry Waters."

She looked up, unable to speak another word due to the rapid beating of her heart and a sudden dearth of breath.

Chester considered this a moment. "He's a polite one, he is."

She quickly folded the note and returned it to her pocket. "I really must be getting back. Myrtle has caused me to get behind making the pies for Lady Tomkins's party."

"Myrtle *is* a behind — if you ask me."

She gave him a smile. "Have a good day, Chester."

On the way back to the shop, Esther roiled against her deception. Yet how could she have read Henry's exact words aloud? They were private. And they would do nothing but hurt Chester.

And Chester didn't deserve to be hurt.

She repeated that fact as she walked. *Chester doesn't deserve to be hurt.*

Chapter Twelve

Esther stared at her reflection, yet saw nothing. Henry was the focus of her mind's eye, meaning her eyes saw no other. She hated that he would miss Verd's party. With the school term starting soon, who knew when she would see him again?

Her thoughts circled back to when she stumbled in the garden and Henry had righted her. How could such a simple act of assistance seem romantic? Yet it was. For in those few moments of contact she'd felt his strength and his caring nature. But more than that, she'd felt a connection, as though by that simple touch they were weaving a bond, like two strands of a rope, winding around each other, being made stronger by the union. A verse came to mind: "'A threefold cord is not quickly broken.'"

Yet she and Henry were only two.

"I am three. I am the first cord. Wind yourselves around Me."

Esther shivered and pressed a hand against her heart. "So Henry is Your choice, Father?"

She waited for an answer, but received none. Yet with one fresh breath and then another, the doubt that had plagued her dissipated. "So Chester is my past and Henry is my future?"

She was shocked by the look of surprise and then calm that passed over her reflection, as if the words had not been mentally formed before they were uttered. She smiled at the knowledge that they — that she — had spoken the truth.

Esther made a vow. "I will speak with Chester after the party. And then write to Henry."

Speaking of, she needed to hurry or she'd be late.

**

Esther arrived at Coventry Hall in Chester's wagon — for they had pies to deliver. She had let Sadie sit in the seat beside Chester, and in spite of their objections, she had sat in back, ostensibly making sure the pies did not slide. But there was another reason for the seating arrangement. To sit so close to Chester when she had all intentions of breaking their engagement was beyond her ability.

Sam opened the door for them — a door that had a fresh coat of paint. He was dressed in fine livery that was a tad too small around the middle. Verd rushed to greet her first guests.

Rush? Verd did not rush.

But the woman took Esther's hands and squeezed them, drawing her into the parlor, leaving Sadie and Chester to deal with the pies. "I am so nervous. This is the first time I have seen the people of Chancebury in eight years since Thomas's funeral procession. And I had little contact before that. Other than having you come visit, I fear I have lost the art of being a hostess. I have hired three village girls to help with the food, and Sam had a lad help with the setting up, so all the logisticals are in place. But as for me. . ."

"Just smile and be yourself." Esther added, "The guests will be nervous, too, for they have never been invited to such a fine house. They will be on their best behavior."

"As will I," came a man's voice.

Henry walked into the room.

Esther nearly swayed at the sight of him.

"I didn't mean to frighten you."

"I am not frightened," she said, regaining her composure. "Only very surprised. You said you could not attend."

Verd pinched his cheek. "I persuaded him to hurry through his work issues as a birthday gift to me." Her pinch turned into a gentle hand against his cheek. "The finest gift I could ever receive."

"You flatter me, Auntie."

"I do no such thing. Now come along you two. Peruse the buffet with me to see if the layout is appealing as well as functional."

They moved through the dining room, out some french doors, and into the garden where tables were already brimming with food. Sadie and Chester were placing the pies with the other delectables: sandwiches, fruit, breads, smoked meat, cheese, and sweets. "The offerings are plenteous," Esther said.

"I hope there is enough."

Esther noticed a mismatch of chairs littering the grounds.

Verd followed her gaze. "I had Sam bring out every chair in the house, yet I know it is not half enough."

Esther laughed at the sight of an ornate French-styled chair with a silk seat set near a simple wooden chair, probably taken from the kitchen. "It is delightful."

"Do you think so? I was hoping the children wouldn't mind sitting on the lawn."

"I am sure they won't mind at all." Henry pointed to the buffet table. "But aren't those stacked dishes your very best Havilland?"

"And my other two sets as well. What is it for, if not to use?"

Esther scanned another table which held crystal goblets, an enormous punch bowl, and forks of fine sterling. "I hope no one snatches a piece."

"Nelly and Sam mentioned that, too," Verd said. "But what are my guests to use if not forks?"

"It will be a temptation to some," Henry said.

"A temptation they will overcome," she said.

"You trust mankind too much."

"God will witness their actions." She shook her head, dismissing the subject. "They are but things. I have lived among things long enough. It is time I live among people — among my neighbors."

Sam appeared in the doorway. "They are arriving, Lady Tomkins."

Verd touched the simple ruby necklace hanging around her neck. "I'm coming."

Esther and Henry followed her in. There was only time enough for Esther to say, "I'm so glad to see you again, Henry."

"You received my note?"

"I did. And I thank you for it."

"I meant every sentiment. Every —"

The first guests flowed into the foyer, their eyes wide as they took in the lush surroundings: the sweeping staircase, the gilt-framed paintings, the intricate pattern in the rugs. Verd turned to Esther, her eyes panicked. "Help them along to the garden, Mrs. Horton. Henry?"

Esther and Henry hurried to her rescue.

**

Esther looked over the garden and grounds that were littered with people eating, talking, and laughing. Children ran along the garden paths, playing tag and hide-and-seek among the lilac bushes and rhododendron. The buffet table had been gleaned of all edibles, and Esther saw Nelly, Sam, and the hired help collecting china, forks, and glasses from every imaginable place. She'd been doing the same, helping as she could. Not because her help was needed as much as it kept her busy and solved the problem of whether she shared a conversation with Henry or Chester. To have them both present caused her nerves to fray like an unhemmed dress.

And it wasn't just their presence that caused her stress. It was the fact that others made no secret of their interest in the trio. Whispers abounded, along with wicked smiles. Myrtle seemed in her element, flitting from this group to that, spreading her mischief.

Esther spotted Chester watching Myrtle. His brow was dipped, his head cocked to the side as if trying to make heads or tails of it. What had he heard? What was there to hear?

His eyes met Esther's, and he came toward her, a question evident on his face.

"Are you enjoying the party?" she asked.

"Yes, yes. It's a fine party. But something's going on. People are looking at me oddly."

"You *are* especially handsome today."

He gave her the look she deserved. "I heard people whispering."

Esther's stomach tightened. "Chancebury always has someone whispering about something."

"But I heard your name mentioned. And Mr. Waters'."

161

Her thoughts traveled from words of self-defense, to words that could break their engagement, once and for all.

Unfortunately, neither set of words found release before they heard Henry call out, "Attention, everyone! Attention."

Conversation quieted.

"I want to thank my dear aunt for inviting us into her home. She is the most gracious, kind, and loving aunt a man could want. I hope you all get to know her as I do. Happy eightieth birthday, Auntie, and may you have many more!"

There were toasts to Lady Tomkins, huzzahs, and applause.

Verd acknowledged their well wishes. "Thank you for coming. I guarantee this will not be my last soiree."

More cheers.

But she wasn't through. "I would also like to make an announcement." She glanced at Henry, then Esther. "I have hopes of opening a school in

Chancebury soon. A school for boys *and* girls."

Really?

Esther looked to Henry. He smiled at her and nodded. Why hadn't they said anything?

The mason's daughter raised a hand. "I could go, too?"

"You could go, too."

Murmurs rustled all around—not all positive—but Verd quieted them. "It is just in a planning phase, but since you are all here, I wanted to share it with you. Again, thank you for coming."

As people began to disperse, Chester quickly stepped forward. "Since we are toasting, I want everyone to raise a glass to my lovely fiancée, Esther. I cannot wait for her to become my wife."

There was applause and shouts of affirmation, but Esther only heard it vaguely, as sounds heard through a wall. What loomed large was the look of shock and betrayal on Verd's face.

Chester linked Esther's arm in his.

The dip in Henry's brow and the pale wash of his skin was a knife to Esther's heart. He came close and shook Chester's hand. "Congratulations." Then he bowed formally to Esther. "Best wishes for the future."

But. . .but. . . Let me explain!

"Now if you will excuse me, I must return to Manchester." He rushed past his aunt.

"Henry?" Verd said.

"I must go, Auntie. I'm sorry."

"Oh dear. I will see you out." With a glare to Esther, she added, "I need to talk to you."

Esther turned to Chester. "Lady Tomkins needs me. I will be right back." She hurried into the house, hoping to catch Henry before he left. But she was moments too late as his horse galloped down the drive.

"But I need to tell him. . .explain. . ."

Verd took her arm none too gently and drew her past the parlor, past the dining room, into a room that served as a pantry. She closed the door.

"You wish to explain. Explain. Immediately," she demanded.

"I didn't know Chester was going to say anything."

"So it's true? You are betrothed?"

Esther focused on a bag of opened flour that had sprinkled on the floor. "It is true. But I. . .I don't want it to be true."

"You hurt Henry. And myself. You betrayed our trust. You know the feelings he has for you."

"To hurt him pains me greatly. Just this morning I made the decision to break my engagement with Chester."

Verd crossed her arms. "You waited too long."

Esther pressed her hands to her face. "It is such a muddle."

"Then do something about it."

"What can I do? Henry has left. The pained look upon his face. . . I will never forget it."

"Nor should you. Tell me this: when did you accept Chester's proposal?"

"At the festival. Last week."

"Why didn't you tell me?"

"I was going to, but then Henry was here, and I discovered he was the man with the wheel — the man who had made me think true love was possible. I was so happy to see him again."

"Some way to show it."

"You know I was happy in his company. I enjoyed talking with him and walking in the garden. . ."

"So you have feelings for Henry?"

"I do. I. . .I love him."

"A disturbing way to show it."

"I was going to tell Chester after the party, and write to Henry. But then he was here and—"

"Good intentions mean little. I thought you were a woman of honor."

"I am. I was trying to be. Chester is a good man, and I hate hurting him."

"So now you've hurt Henry."

"I didn't mean to. I was going to sort it all out today."

"Too little, too late." Verd flipped a hand at her. "I must say goodbye to my guests."

"May I come by tomorrow and talk? Help me repair this. Please."

"I see no repair to this, Mrs. Horton. Do not come again."

She left Esther alone in the pantry. With her pain. And her guilt.

**

Chester stopped the wagon in front of Esther's. "I'm sorry for your headache. I was hoping to come in."

"Not tonight." *I've caused enough pain for one day.* She watched as Sadie moved from the back of the wagon to the seat beside him. "See you in the morning, Sadie."

Esther went into her cottage but kept the candles unlit. She made her way to her room and fell upon the bed, fully clothed. She pulled a pillow close, hugged it, and prayed the pain of losing her best friend *and* the love of her life would subside.

Knowing very well it wouldn't.

Chapter Thirteen

First Chester. Then Verd.

That was the order of the day. Break her engagement with Chester, then mend her relationship with Verd.

As for Henry? He was gone. His reaction to her engagement proved his feelings for her. Deceived, he had left with a broken heart. Could his heart be mended? There was no way to know. But either way, Esther knew she could not marry Chester.

She reached the smithy, but he was not there.

"Where is Mr. Mayfield?" she asked his helper.

"In the barn, ma'am. A horse is foaling."

She detoured to the barn and heard commotion inside. She didn't want to intrude, nor was she comfortable seeing the process. Instead, she peeked through an opened window.

She was surprised to see Sadie with Chester, helping with the birth.

Her second reaction was anger. He'd called Sadie in to help and not her?

He knows of your squeamishness. He knows you care little for horses.

Logic calmed her reaction. She sat on a trough to wait.

As Chester and Sadie — and the mare — worked, she could hear them discussing horses. Esther had never known of Sadie's fondness for them. *What else don't I know?*

Suddenly, there was a lot of commotion, and then exclamations of joy. "There she is!"

Esther peeked through the window a second time and saw the newborn foal in the straw. Chester and Sadie laughed and congratulated each other.

Then Chester asked Sadie, "What's your middle name?"

"Matilda."

"Then I will name the new foal Mattie, after you."

Sadie awkwardly hugged him. "Thank you."

Esther's throat tightened at the touching moment. There was a definite connection between them. But what made it even more telling was the knowledge that there was no such connection between herself and Chester. Their affection was amiable enough, but matched to what she'd just witnessed, it was a shallow stream compared to a mighty river.

And then, in a rush, all of Sadie's half-hearted support for Esther and Chester's engagement came to mind. Plus her utter joy when she'd danced with him at the festival. And her quick smile and her penchant for coming out of the oven room every time he came in the shop.

Could it be. . . ? Did Sadie feel romantic affection for him?

"Open your eyes and see what I have done."

Had God brought them together? Beyond a flash of jealousy, Esther's thoughts moved to a different avenue: Could Sadie's feelings for Chester be a way to soften the blow of Esther breaking their engagement?

She heard Sadie say, "I need to get to the shop. I started the ovens before I came, but Esther will be wondering where I am."

Esther knew she couldn't speak to Chester just yet. She had to speak to someone else first.

She hurried to the shop.

**

"I'm sorry I'm late," Sadie said as she came in just moments behind Esther. She pointed to the ovens. "I was here, but then I got called away."

Esther measured some flour for a crust. "It must have been something important for you to leave."

Sadie tied on her apron. "It was. Chester stopped by in a tizzy. Annabelle was foaling."

The simple fact that Sadie knew the name of Chester's horse—and Esther didn't—loomed large. "You went to help?"

Her face glowed with the memory of it. "To see a birth like that. . ." She beamed.

"He named her after me—after my middle name, Matilda."

"That's very kind of him."

"Yes, well. . ." She looked away. "Chester is a very kind man."

Father, let the truth come out. "You two have a special bond."

Sadie hedged. "Perhaps we do."

"I saw it."

"You did?"

"When Mattie was born. I was outside."

Sadie looked embarrassed. "We do have a connection, but don't worry. . ."

Esther had to ask the difficult question. "Do you care for him? Beyond friendship?"

Sadie stepped toward the oven room.

Esther caught her arm. "Do you? Don't worry about what I might think about it, tell the truth."

Sadie's face battled a storm of emotions. Finally she said, "I do. I know I shouldn't because he's yours, but. . .but I do. I love him." She took a new breath and said more softly, "I do."

Esther was silent a moment, gauging how she felt about this new knowledge. She expected to feel regret or anger. She did not expect to feel relief. "How long have you loved him?"

"Since always. And we might have been married, too, but when your husband died, Chester turned his sights on you and made winning your hand a quest. I didn't have a chance."

"Does he know how you feel?"

Sadie shook her head. "He only has eyes for you. I do everything I possibly can to make him know I care, but he doesn't see it."

It was time for Esther to share her truth. "I don't want to marry him."

"Since when?"

Since Henry. But it was more than Henry. "Chester is a decent man—a very persistent man. He wore down my defenses until I agreed."

Sadie bit her lip. "What are we doing to do?"

"There is only one thing we can do, and I must start the process."

"By. . . ?"

"By breaking our engagement."

Sadie's face brightened then grew serious. "It will hurt him. He's wanted you for so long."

"But you love him."

"That doesn't mean he loves me or would marry me, even if he was free. Love often comes unbidden. I didn't mean to love him."

As I didn't mean to love Henry. And just because Esther was free didn't mean Henry would come back to her.

"We must take the risk, Sadie. True love is a gift from God, but love that is lacking in truth offends Him." By making this choice, Esther knew she might end up without a man. Yet being alone was preferable to living a lie.

She remembered her gleeful "I'm free!" moment after Petunia married. She could be alone and happy. Perhaps God wanted her alone.

Hopefully not.

Esther extended a hand toward Sadie. "Let us pray all works out exactly as the Almighty wishes it to."

"And may God give you the words to kindly tell Chester it's over."

Amen.

Esther waited for Chester to come in for his daily pie. When he didn't and she saw the stable boy running by outside, she hurried out of the shop to stop him.

"Hey, boy. Where are you going so fast?"

"Mr. Mayfield slipped off a ladder and sprained his ankle bad. I'm going for me ma. She knows about such things."

Esther knew nothing about such things, but she said, "I'll go."

Sadie stepped out to the square. "No. I know what to do. I'll go." She looked at Esther. "Yes?"

Absolutely. As Esther watched Sadie hurry off with the boy, she knew she had witnessed God in action. He had opened a door for Sadie. It was a chance for the bond between her and Chester to deepen. And as such, God had shown Esther her own door. And closed it. *Please do Your work, Lord. Let everything fall into place as only You can.*

Sadie returned at midday. Esther was glad to see her assistant because she herself had burned the first pie. But she was also glad to see her because she was desperate to know what had happened.

And how Chester was doing, of course. Yet that seemed secondary. For if God was behind all this, Chester's sprained ankle was a part of His handiwork. God would take care of Chester's injury. As He would take care of Chester. And Sadie. And Esther.

As soon as the ovens were stoked to Sadie's satisfaction, she came into the main part of the shop.

"Well?" Esther asked.

"Firstly, Chester will be fine."

"I'm glad. But give me more."

Sadie grinned. "He said I was a very special lady."

"You are. He is wise to see it."

"We talked about Mattie."

"He was happy to see you then?"

"He was."

"Did he ask where I was?"

"Well. . .no."

Esther beat down her disappointment. Her pride was injured while her hope was curried. "It's time, then?"

"For you to speak to him?"

Esther nodded. "I'll bring him his pie." She removed her apron. "Wish me luck."

"You have it. And my prayers."

**

"So you see, I don't want either of us to settle for what could be. I want us to find the kind of love that should be. That has to be."

Chester sat in a chair, his right foot on a stool. He stared at his fireplace, though in the late summer heat there was no fire. "I was wondering about that."

"About love?"

"About our sort of love. It just didn't seem. . ." He searched for the word. "Full enough." He stroked his chin. "Kind of like a pie that's got half the pieces missing."

Esther laughed. "I can think of no better analogy."

The deed was done, and Esther offered God a silent thank-you.

But there was more to be accomplished.

"Sadie told me about Mattie."

"She was a big help to me."

"Then and with your ankle."

He looked at his ankle as if studying it. "She's a very good woman."

"The best." She wondered if she should say more. And then she said it. "She loves you."

"What?"

"She always has, but I got in the way."

"She always has?"

He was like a lad being told a girl fancied him. Esther could have stayed but felt it was time to leave. Let Chester work through the rest on his own.

She leaned down and kissed his forehead. "I do love you, Chester, as a dear and trusted friend. I wish you the best always."

He grabbed her hand and kissed it. "As I do for you, Esther."

As she left Esther remembered her "What now?" question after Petunia had married. She'd thought the answer was to marry Chester. Now that door was closed. So once again she asked God, "What now?"

The answer was unknown. Yet Esther Horton did not simply walk away from Chester's. She flew on the wings of hope, and the assurance that God was in control.

**

Esther was greeted at the door by Nelly. "Lady Tomkins does not wish to see you, Mrs. Horton."

"Tell her it's imperative I speak with her. Essential." She saw Christopher walking out of the parlor and suspected Verd was sitting nearby. Esther raised her voice. "Tell her I am despicable and deserve her wrath. I come to her, asking forgiveness. If she values our friendship at all, I beg her to—"

"Gracious!" Verd called out from the parlor. "If you are taking the route of confession and absolution at least give me the satisfaction of being a full witness."

Nelly rolled her eyes as she let Esther enter. As expected, Verd was sitting in her usual place. Esther stood directly in front of her. "Good afternoon, Lady Tomkins."

"It's Verd to you."

Esther smiled.

Verd pointed at her. "Do not smile. One does not smile while groveling."

"Does one sit?"

"I'd prefer a full kneel, but yes, I suppose you can sit and grovel."

Esther pulled a chair close and sat with her hands clasped in her lap. "I am truly and utterly sorry I hurt you."

"And my nephew."

"Especially him."

Her eyebrow rose. "So he takes precedence over me?"

"In this sin, yes, he does. For I hurt you by a sin of omission in not telling you that Chester and I were engaged."

"Indeed you did."

"I meant to tell you on the day Henry stepped into the room. But once I met him. . ."

Verd's eyebrow rose again. "Yes?"

A thousand words stood by, waiting their turn. "I have never met anyone like Henry. When I saw his face during that first meeting on the road, my heart shifted." She clutched her hands to her chest. "I can honestly say I have not stopped thinking of him since."

"He is a memorable man."

"He is. You arranged for us to spend time together—and I knew your intent and did not set it right by being honest with you. In truth, I enjoyed our time so immensely that I chose to ignore what was real for this lofty other-world that existed when I was with Henry." She gazed into her friend's eyes with full intensity. "He ignites something in me that makes me see more, be more, and want more."

"Little good it will do since you're marrying Chester."

Finally, the good news. "I broke my engagement right before I came here."

Verd sat taller. "How did he react?"

"He was more gracious than I deserved."

"I believe that."

Esther accepted the barb. "I still see the horrified look on Henry's face when Chester toasted our engagement. To love him yet see him hurt like that. . . Will he ever forgive me for hurting him?"

"You will have to ask him."

"When is he — ?"

Suddenly, Henry stepped into the room.

Esther stood, her heart racing. "You're here."

"I am. I rode away in anger, but I returned."

Verd beckoned him closer. "Tell her why you returned."

He extended his hands to Esther. She felt tears threaten as she anticipated, hoped, and prayed for what would come next. She took his hands, forming a circle between them.

"I returned because I was not willing to let you go so easily. Without a fight."

"Really?"

"And?" Verd said. "Get to the point, boy."

"The point is, I love you. I adore you." He lowered to one knee. "Esther, would you do me the great honor of becoming my wife?"

"Yes! Oh yes!"

Their embrace was accompanied by Verd's applause.

And God's. For Esther felt God's blessings encircle them. "Thank You, Lord," she whispered against Henry's shoulder.

He let go enough to see her face. "I agree, my darling. For you are an answer to prayer."

Esther touched his lovely face, the face that had made her love him at first sight.

He gazed into her eyes. "Remember when we first met, I asked if you'd come to save me?"

"I do."

"I believe you've done just that. For I have been saved from a life made lonely by your absence."

"As you have saved me, dear love. As you have saved me."

Epilogue

Henry stood in Coventry Hall in his uncle's old study, a room commandeered to a new use as the Chancebury Academy of Learning. It was a scholarly room with three walls lined with walnut shelving that held a treasure of books about subjects from horticulture; to the strategy of war; to the classics of Plato, Descartes, Shakespeare, and of course, Daniel Defoe. For what child could grow up without reading *Robinson Crusoe*? If that story didn't ignite the imaginations of the students, nothing would.

Henry had repositioned his uncle's desk so it was at the opposite end, facing the books. In between were long tables and benches that would seat five children in four rows. Positioned at each place was a slate, chalk, a rag for erasing, and a copy of *The Protestant Tutor*, which would teach the children their alphabet, with a few morals thrown in for good measure.

Esther set the last book. "There. We are ready."

"Their places and supplies are ready, but am I?"

She went to him and gave a kiss. "This is a good thing we're doing, Henry. For many children, this may be the only schooling they ever receive."

"Do not add to the burden of my responsibility, wife."

"I will be here to help."

He drew her hand around his arm. "Will you miss the pie shop?"

"Not a bit, for it is in good hands. Sadie knows more about making pies than I do."

"And Chester is made glad for the free lifetime supply."

Esther was ecstatic for her own marriage, but also for the marriage of Sadie and Chester. It was unfortunate they'd had the wedding while she and Henry were on their honeymoon, but there had been no reason for them to wait. Life was short. Best grab onto happiness as soon as possible.

"I am eager for the maps we purchased in Italy to arrive," Henry said.

"And the etchings of the masterworks. We did well in Florence. And Rome. And Paris. And Vienna."

He looked down at her and winked. "Very well."

She felt herself blush.

Suddenly, he patted his vest pocket. "Oh dear. I forgot my watch."

"I'll fetch it. I will be but a minute." Another change in their lives had been moving into Coventry Hall. There were obviously rooms enough, and Verd appreciated the company and was very good about giving the newlyweds their privacy.

Esther was leaving to get the watch when she heard young voices in the foyer. "They're here," she whispered.

"May God have mercy on our souls!"

Esther stepped back as Verd entered the study with a little girl on each hand. "Here we are, children." Four boys streamed in behind, their eyes scanning the room in awe.

"Crikey," said the oldest, who looked about ten. "I didn't know so many books were in the whole, entire world."

"Take a seat, everyone," Esther said.

Verd flicked one of them on the nose. "I will see to the scones and milk."

"We get to eat, too?" a girl asked.

"It is a known fact that learning is enhanced by a full belly," Verd said as she left.

Just then five more were ushered in by Sam. Fourteen students. A goodly number.

A godly number.

Henry clapped to get their attention. "Welcome to the wonderful and amazing world of learning, children."

A wonderful and amazing world indeed.

THE END

About the Author

NANCY MOSER is the best-selling author of over 40 novels, novellas, and children's books, including Christy Award winner *Time Lottery* and Christy finalist *Washington's Lady*. She's written seventeen historical novels including *Love of the Summerfields*, *Masquerade*, *Where Time Will Take Me*, and *Just Jane*. *An Unlikely Suitor* was named to Booklist's "Top 100 Romance Novels of the Decade." *The Pattern Artist* was a finalist in the Romantic Times Reviewers Choice award. Some of her contemporary novels are: *An Undiscovered Life*, *The Invitation*, *Solemnly Swear*, *The Good Nearby*, *John 3:16*, *Crossroads*, *The Seat Beside Me*, and the Sister Circle series. *Eyes of Our Heart* was a finalist in the Faith, Hope, and Love Readers' Choice Awards. Nancy has been married for over 45 years—to the same man. She and her husband have three grown children, seven grandchildren, and live in the Midwest. She's been blessed with a varied life. She's earned a degree in architecture, run a business with her husband, traveled extensively in Europe, and has performed in various theaters, symphonies, and choirs. She knits voraciously, kills all her houseplants, and can wire an electrical fixture without getting shocked. She is a fan of anything antique—humans included.

Website: www.nancymoser.com

Blogs: Author blog:
www.authornancymoser.blogspot.com History
blog: www.footnotesfromhistory.blogspot.com

Facebook:
www.facebook.com/nancymoser.author

Bookbub: www.bookbub.com/authors/nancy-moser?list=author_ books

Goodreads:
www.goodreads.com/author/show/117288.Nancy_Moser

Pinterest:
www.pinterest.com/nancymoser1/_saved/

Instagram: www.instagram.com/nmoser33/

If you love Regency stories,
read about the queen of Regency,
read the story of Jane Austen's life as
told by Jane herself!

Excerpt from *Just Jane*

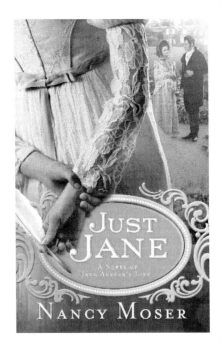

It is a true thing everyone knows that —

I scratch out the words, dip my pen into the well of ink, and try again.

It's not the first time I've scribbled and scratched, obliterating one word or phrase while searching for another. I long for the correct word, the indisputable one-and-only connection of words that will capture the essence of my intention. Yet these unfound words tease me by hiding in the shadows of my mind, just out of reach, being naughty and bothersome and—

Aha!

I quickly put pen to paper, eager to capture the phrase before it returns to hiding: *It is a truth universally acknowledged* . . . Yes, yes, that is the phrase that's eluded me. I dip the pen again, finally ready to complete the part of the sentence that has never been in question.

. . . that a single man in possession of a good fortune, must be in want of a wife.

I sit back in my chair, feeling absurdly prideful that I've completed this one line. And yet, it's an important line. The first line of a book. Actually, it's not a book yet. Would it ever by chance be a book?

I peer out the window of the rectory. My mother is bent over her beloved garden, plucking weeds from her asters and lavender hydrangea. *I should go help her.*

But I don't want to. Mine is not a penchant for plantings and pinchings, but for pronouns and prepositions.

Mother stands and arches her back. I suffer her moan without hearing it. She looks in my direction and I offer a wave, which she returns. A lesser—or would it be grander?— mother would observe the gaze of a child who possesses two able hands, and immediately summon her outside to assist with the work. But my dear mother (and father too), in spite of having no necessity to do so, condone and even encourage my writing. That it will never amount to anything, that the eyes of family will be the only eyes that will fall upon my carefully chosen "truth universally acknowledged" is also recognized and accepted, yet ignored as unimportant.

"Express yourself, dear child," has always been an invocation in the

Austen household, and my sister, Cassandra (two years my elder), and my six brothers (all but one older than I) have always been eager to embrace the unspoken possibilities enmeshed within our parents' appeal. We do our best to be who we might be — in all our grace, geniality, and glib foolery. That some are more glib and fool than graceful and genial is also not considered a complete disgrace. A person content to be bland will never be anyone's first choice as a companion for an idle afternoon.

Mother goes back to work, releasing me from any hint of guilt. I return to my rich gentleman in want of a wife. If only it were true. We Englishwomen of 1795 have no recourse but to assume it is so. Pray it is so. For how else will we ever prosper? Cassandra and I often huddle together in our shared bed, whispering in the darkness about the inequities of inheritance. How unfair that only the male of the species is permitted to inherit. Alas, the females of our world — if they don't find themselves a willing rich man — are bequeathed a life of obligation, forever beholden to the kind heart of some charitable relative to provide a roof that does not leak, a fireplace that does not smoke, and a meal that might occasionally contain meat. Such is our lot if we don't marry well.

I myself can say with some measure of pride that at age twenty, I have prospects. Or at least one prospect. And after all, a woman only needs but one if he be the right one. His name is Tom Lefroy. He is a charming Irishman, the nephew of a neighbour I saw at a ball last Christmas. His eyes are as blue as the Hampshire sky. . . .

We danced every dance. When he took my hand to instigate a cross, rather than merely letting my hand sit gently upon his own, he squeezed it with subtle meaning. And when we slid by, one past the other, shoulder passing shoulder, we didn't look straight ahead, as others with less intent would do, but turned our heads inward, our chins glancing upon our shoulders as our eyes glanced upon each other. With but an instant for conversation, we resorted to single words, words full of teasing. And entreaty.

"Beautiful," he whispered as his shoulder skimmed mine.

"Rascal," was my reply next pass.

"Determined." He offered a wink.

"Ambitious."

The dance proceeded to other movements, silencing our verbal banter. Two dozen couples rose up on their toes, then lowered themselves to just height as they swept up and back, not one step missed, all ably immersed in the elegance of a common sway and parry.

To others it may have been a lark, an amusement on a cold December evening, but for Tom and me it was a sparring, a deliberate caracole, turning, ever turning toward each other and away, despairing of steps that forced time and space between us. I became heady with the sustained implication, as well as the anticipation of more.

But suddenly, as one dance ended and the musicians began the prelude for another, Tom took my hand and said, "Let's hide away."

He pulled me into the foyer, to a

bench leaning back against the wall of the mighty staircase but slightly hidden by a tall stand set with a porcelain urn. We fell onto the seat, a jumble of conspiracy, motion, and laughter.

"There," he said, setting himself aright. "Now I have you where I want you."

Before I had time to respond, he leaned forward and kissed me. . .

I put my fingers to my lips, hoping their light pressure will help me remember the one and only...

I admit that Tom and I behaved in a most shocking manner, dancing with no thought or eyes to another, sitting down together, head to head, knee to knee, discussing Tom Jones, and laughing in a way that caused many a matronly stare. That we didn't care was shameless. Yet I would not change one moment of our time — which was too fleeting.

Before the third ball, I visited the Lefroy home in Ashe on the auspices of visiting Tom's aunt Anne, a dear friend. Of course, I had hoped to see

Tom . . . just to see him would have fed and sustained me, like partaking in one meal, all the while knowing there will be another.

But Tom had fled the house—as if avoiding me? And though I enjoyed my visit with Anne, it didn't hold the delicious delicacies I'd expected. I now hold on to the hope that Tom was truly called away. Or did he flee because his family teased him about our attraction? Families can be relentless and cruel even as they try to be delightful.

The next day, my feast was complete, as Tom came to call. The presence of his little cousin George was not the ideal— and was a surprise I didn't quite understand—but I was so pleased to partake of Tom's company that I told myself I didn't mind. And yet . . . I sigh when I allow myself to imagine the meeting I would have desired versus the one that transpired with a thirteen-year-old chaperon who talked about nonsense when I wanted to talk about . . . other things of far more import.

When a fourth ball was planned at Ashe, I held hopes that it was called to honour our upcoming match. In my anticipation I prepared many sets of dialogue that revealed how I would have the evening play out. Tom and I would return to our own special corner behind the urn. As he made his intentions known, he would combine his wit and charm with an eloquence that would impress me to such a degree that I would find myself willing to marry him just in hopes of hearing such eloquence again. And again.

Ah, the burdens of imagination . . . when the evening didn't play out according to my carefully created dialogue and staging, my disappointment grew to such an extent that others asked of my infirmity. I found a quiet hall and gave myself a good talking to, faulting myself, chiding myself. . . . For in spite of my intense wishes, it's a known fact that people are not characters in a story, bidden by my whim to act and be according to how I wish them to act and be.

A few days after this fourth ball,

dear Tom was sent away to London to continue his law studies. He had spoken of them, so I was not surprised. Not completely surprised. He had also spoken of the pressures of being the oldest male of his generation. His father had married for love and lost his inheritance and, as such, had no fortune to pass along. But Tom's great-uncle Benjamin in London . . . ah, there is *the* fortune he needs to cultivate. It's the prudent thing to do for Tom's future — and mine. It's not unusual for the responsibilities and expectations of his gender to take precedent over the needs and desires of a young female with aspiring plans of her own. One's future must be nurtured and finalized to the best of one's ability, in fate's time, not ours.

Yet even with my dashed expectations at the final ball, and my disappointment in Tom's leaving, I take heart in knowing that our initial banter had grown to include some measure of substance. Enough substance that a future together is more than just a girlish inkling or a plot in a story.

And my expectations *are* recognized beyond my own hopeful wishes. My brother Henry's friend, who was here to visit over Christmas, presented me with a portrait of Tom, drawn by his own hand, assuming, of course, that I would delight in it. Which I do. I hold on to that portrait, as it is the only Tom I've seen during these ten long months he has been gone. I expect him to visit our home in Steventon soon, with the proposition to share our future forthcoming. He will go far, my Tom, and I will be a good wife.

I think of him, the oldest boy, the eldest son of twelve children, with five older sisters. . . .

Five older sisters . . . all in want of a husband.

Female names interrupt my thoughts of Tom, listing themselves as though they are real and have but to make my acquaintance: Elizabeth, Jane, Mary, Lydia, and Catherine—no, Kitty. . . . I nod, accepting their introduction, for each seems just right.

Five girls, each in want of a husband. Is this how I can dislodge my story from its hard-fought first line? I will begin with the sisters discussing their lot, chattering over the need for a gentleman who is, of course, in need of them. . . .

It's as good a place as any to begin. At a beginning.

Made in United States
North Haven, CT
22 March 2022

17431744R00121